Bolan scanned the terrain left and right

Four two-man teams on both flanks were cautiously moving forward in search of Fowler's mercenaries. Their steady pace would keep them alive, but wouldn't allow them to cut off the hardmen before they entrenched themselves in the mountain fortress.

Molembe had lowered his radio pack. A few moments later he cradled the handset.

"What's the damage?" Bolan asked, still searching the horizon with the binoculars.

"We lost contact with two choppers. A third got caught in the dust storm and crashed. All this and the fight hasn't even begun."

"It has now!" Bolan shoved Molembe to the ground. The first shot zipped into the sand next to the Executioner, the second and third digging into the ground where Molembe had been standing. Then the Desert Knights opened up with everything they had.

MACK BOLAN®

The Executioner

DON PENDLETON'S

THE EXECUTIONER

FEATURING MACK BOLAN

WARRIOR'S EDGE

A GOLD EAGLE BOOK FROM

WORLDWIDE

TORONTO • NEW YORK • LONDON
AMSTERDAM • PARIS • SYDNEY • HAMBURG
STOCKHOLM • ATHENS • TOKYO • MILAN
MADRID • WARSAW • BUDAPEST • AUCKLAND

First edition July 1992

ISBN 0-373-61163-3

Special thanks and acknowledgment to
Rich Rainey for his contribution to this work.

WARRIOR'S EDGE

Printed in U.S.A.

It is a fearful thing to lead this great peaceful people into war.... But the right is more precious than peace, and we shall fight for the things we have always carried nearest our hearts—for democracy, for the right of those who submit to authority to have a voice in their own government.

—Woodrow Wilson
August 19, 1914

I'd be the first to say that armed aggression rarely solves anything. But when a tinpot despot seeks to destroy the tender beginnings of the democratic process, it's time to stand up and strike a blow for freedom.

—Mack Bolan

1

The battered kepi lay flat on the sand, its torn brim stained with sweat and blood. There was no sign of the owner, no tracks. The dust storm that had swept over the Harana Desert for the past hour had seen to that. It looked as if the legionnaire had been swallowed by the desert sands.

Bolan's lean shadow blocked the cap from the hot afternoon sun as he approached and crouched beside it. The warrior felt parched and baked, his entire body sandpapered by stinging grit from the dust storm that had come up suddenly and separated him and his companions from their quarry. It had forced the two-man hunting teams to take shelter for the duration of the storm. Like crabs they'd burrowed into the sand and clay until the whirlwinds died down.

The storm had hit at the worst possible time, almost as if the outlaw mercenaries had someone up above looking out for them.

But Bolan knew that the man who led the mercenary army was no Moses. The only deity looking out for Heinrich Fowler was the god of war. Not that Fowler was a god-fearing man. The only higher power he believed in came from the end of a gun—power he and his Desert Knights exercised at every opportunity.

Bolan scanned the area. Other than the kepi, there was no sign of human traffic. But at least they were on the right track. The outlaw mercs were still moving east.

The Executioner walked back to the last steep sand ridge he'd traversed. As he neared the crest, he crouched and looked toward the horizon, seeing nothing but dry desert terrain, ridges of dust-blanketed rock and, now and then, small green islands of scrub brush.

He shouted once.

Nothing.

He shouted again, and the sand took shape about fifty yards away from him.

Martin Molembe's sand-colored camouflage form gradually rose above the horizon, silhouetted for a brief moment as he came over the dune.

Like Bolan, he'd rolled his sand-colored bandanna into a sweatband beneath the brim of the desert cap that shielded his regal face from the sun.

Molembe was an expert tracker, but he was more than just a hunter. He was also a man used to command. As the current head of the Zandesi Intelligence Service—ZIS—Molembe had been one of the pillars of the new government, putting his life on the line so that free elections could be held in the West African country of Zandesi.

Unfortunately the new government had been literally stolen by Heinrich Fowler—the last of a clan of petty tyrants who refused to give up what he'd gained through murder and fear—and was a government in involuntary exile, hidden somewhere in the desert.

Molembe had personally coordinated the two-man search parties, making sure he was teamed up with Bolan.

The Executioner was under no illusions. Though Molembe said he wanted to work with the American operative, there was another reason. He also wanted to watch him. To Molembe, Bolan was an unproved commodity who could be just as treacherous as the mercenaries they were pursuing.

Bolan shielded his eyes and watched the tall Zandesian approach, his heavy weight moving gracefully across the shifting sand.

Ever since the two men had resumed their search, they'd been drifting in and out of each other's sight, but they always stayed within hailing distance.

It was the same way all the way down the line.

Several other two-man units were patrolling the area, spread out in search of the Desert Knights. It was hard going on foot, but the trackers had no choice. They had to leave their Land Rovers at the edge of the huge sand pan that the fleeing mercs had driven straight into. Their jeeps and flatbeds had cracked through the thin crust and into the mud below. Tombstone radiators stuck out of the sand, mired until some heavy equipment could pluck the mercenaries' vehicles from the harsh desert cemetery.

Then the mercs had continued on foot.

By the time the trackers had caught up to the sandpan graveyard, Fowler's men had a good head start into the Zandesian wasteland. The previous year's drought had turned most of the Harana Desert into a patchwork of dried riverbeds, dunes and desert plains. Only a few permanent water holes remained.

Between rainy seasons it was as hospitable as Mars. But if they wanted to find the Desert Knights and the captive president of Zandesi, the trackers had to traverse that alien environment.

"What have you found?" Martin Molembe asked as he neared Bolan, his rhythmic steps pistoning through the sand.

The African's angular face was covered with sweat, but he showed no signs of fatigue. He was the kind of man who would go full bore every step of the way until it was physically impossible to take another step. And then he'd drop.

Bolan uncapped his canteen and wet his lips slightly, then nodded toward the kepi in the sand.

"You found John Bandu," Molembe said, a touch of hope coloring his heavy bass voice.

"Not unless he shrunk and hid under that hat," Bolan replied. "Take a closer look. My guess is that there won't be much of him left to find."

The ZIS chief stepped down the ridge, the hissing sand shifting from his mountainous weight, and crouched beside the kepi.

Then he saw the blood. "It's John's," he said. "Head of the presidential bodyguards."

Former head bodyguard, Bolan thought. "How do you know who it belonged to?"

"The rest of the president's men wore plain clothes, but John always wore his uniform. He was always on guard. Always ready to give his life..."

"Looks like Fowler took it." The Executioner saw no need to mince words.

Unlike the lush tropical environment along Zandesi's West African coastline where most of the population lived, the desert was punishing. It took a lot out of a man, made small things crucial. Life often depended on the slightest change in temperature. The endless sun and sand could drive a man mad.

The Executioner had to see how the Zandesian reacted to death under these circumstances, which could well determine whether the two men went on living. If he was a hothead given to maniacal rages, then Bolan would go it alone. If not, maybe they could work together.

But Molembe kept his emotions in check, though it pained him to realize that his friend's chances of survival were slim.

The broad-shouldered tracker shook his head, then dropped the kepi back onto the sand. His face hardened and his eyes narrowed.

Then he moved on without saying a word.

They scoured the stretch of flat land that lay before the next ridge, their weapons leading the way as they approached the rise.

They moved slowly and quietly, the sun blazing down on them and casting mirage lines on the horizon.

Eventually they found John Bandu.

He was waiting for them just past the next ridge, lying flat on his back, sprawled out on the slope. His wrists were tied by thick cords of twine that bound him to the sparlike remains of a bleached acacia tree.

Bloodred holes crisscrossed his body, carved by merciless volleys of automatic fire. The wounds were legion, his legs, hips, chest and arms reduced to a sickening rubble of bone and blood. Only his face was intact, although his forehead was bruised and bloody.

His eyes stared skyward, totally devoid of moisture.

It had been a slow death.

"The bastards used him for target practice," Bolan growled.

"It's no surprise," Martin said, kneeling beside the dead man. With a flash of steel he cut him free from his bonds. Then he touched his palm to his forehead while speaking softly in the French patois common in West Africa.

Like a final benediction he lowered his hand to Bandu's eyes. The eyelids were dry and rough, but finally they slid down. "He goes to a better place," Molembe stated.

"What kind of men are these?"

The Zandesian looked hard at Bolan. "Colonials," he finally replied. "White warriors who come here like gods to treat other men like cattle. Or use them for sport."

The man spoke matter-of-factly, his deep voice holding a careful measure of controlled rage that stemmed from years of living under colonial-backed regimes. He'd never accepted that corrupt rule, but he'd survived it. Just as he'd survived Heinrich Fowler's backstage reign. Now, unless they recovered the presidential party, he might have to survive it again.

Bolan hadn't really expected a response. The answer was all too clear. The mercenaries they pursued were outlaws. As long as there were no witnesses, they figured a gun was a license to kill. A license they exercised at every opportunity.

Though he'd never seen Heinrich Fowler in the flesh, he'd seen him in spirit often enough. The mercenary world was full of his kind. Bolan had gone against them in every part of the globe.

The warrior gestured toward the body. "The men responsible for this might turn on the president at any time."

"No," Molembe replied. "Fowler's a beast, but he's a cunning one. He has plenty of others to take out his fury on. If need be, he'll start killing his own. But he won't hurt the president. Not yet."

Bolan nodded. He knew of Fowler only by reputation and by his briefing from Hal Brognola. Molembe knew him personally, and his deeds were imprinted on his memory.

They studied the terrain. Ahead of them was a dried riverbed, and beyond lay a hard-crusted valley ringed by plateaus, ridges and small mountains. There was no sign of the mercs, but that was to be expected. The mountain range held limitless places to hide.

Molembe gestured toward a rocky peak in the shape of a buttress.

"They're probably heading for Mont Bataille. For years it has been the refuge of outlaws. A natural fortress, almost impregnable to assault once they get in place."

"Just as hostile to its inhabitants as its invaders."

The African looked surprised. "You know its history?"

The Executioner shrugged. "I'd be a fool not to." Brognola's briefing had given him sufficient background on the West African country. Mont Bataille had been a battleground since ancient times, when the tribes first worked out their spheres of influence. Those on the outs invariably went into the mountain strongholds, fighting guerrilla wars until they could take over the lusher lands and the ore-laden mining zones.

In turn the new rulers would face attacks from the mountain groups.

That pattern continued until the Europeans arrived to refine the rites of repression. The French and Germans, the British and the Belgians had all staked their claims. Slave labor gave way to work crews, but the lot in life changed little. Men with money owned the Zandesian rank and file, while a few Zandesians grew rich on the arrangement.

The world wars changed things slightly, but not much. After Germany was defeated both times, its grip on the government loosened and its holdings decreased, though there were always a few holdouts like the Fowler clan, who would survive no matter who ruled.

Now French and English were the most common languages spoken in Zandesi, the languages of commerce and conquest. Each nation left its legacy, a colonial past that was never too far from the Zandesian mind.

Neither was war, which seemed almost like a natural condition.

Bolan fielded the glasses and scanned left and right, picking out a few more two-man teams on both flanks who were cautiously nosing forward in search of the mercs.

The slow but steady pace would keep them alive, but probably wouldn't give them time to cut off the hardmen before they entrenched themselves in the mountain fortress.

Fortresses, Bolan corrected himself. The ancient ruins ahead of them had been used as hideouts and strongholds for two thousand years. Castle facades carved from cliff-side rocks. Caves. Trenches. It was a formidable redoubt.

"I'd say it's time we called in a taxi," Bolan said. Turning, he saw that the Zandesian security chief was literally on the same wavelength.

Molembe had already lowered his radio pack and was cradling the handset. A few moments later he contacted Serpentine Force, the ten-unit chopper squadron that made up about fifty percent of the Zandesi Air Force. The remaining air force crafts were a mixture of old cargo planes and fighters, which were usually grounded for repairs since many of the ancient parts were hard-to-find prized artifacts.

Bolan listened while the security chief spoke with the commander of Serpentine Six, the lead copter scouting the Harana Desert.

"They're on their way," Molembe said after breaking contact. "What's left of them."

"What's the damage?" Bolan asked, still scanning the horizon through the glasses.

"We lost contact with two choppers. A third got caught in the dust storm and crashed. All this and the fight hasn't even begun."

"It has now!" Bolan lurched to the left, grabbed the Zandesian's shoulder and flung him off his feet. Molembe tumbled to the ground, his eyes wide with surprise as Bolan hit the dirt next to him.

The first shot zipped into the sand where Bolan had been standing a moment ago, the second and third digging into the ground where Molembe had been positioned.

The cracks of rifle fire accelerated as the Desert Knights opened up with everything they had, unleashing a blizzard of metal rain from their riverbed position. Muzzle-flashes sparked, running up and down the narrow trench formation formed by the dead watercourse.

Echoes of the first barrage gradually faded away, with isolated shots cutting the air around them as Bolan and the Zandesian tracker inched across the sand toward cover.

"We found the devils!" Molembe shouted, dropping behind a pedestal of hard clay and scrub.

"Yeah. We almost found them the hard way." Only the sudden flurry of movement he'd seen through the binoculars had kept them from joining the slain legionnaire on his eternal exodus.

Face close to the ground, Bolan belly-crawled across the ridge, hands and feet pushing at sand and stone until he reached a low, flat altar-shaped sheet of rock.

Lead hail chinked into the other side of the rock, then thudded up the ridge. The gunners weren't sure where Bolan and his companion were or if they'd been hit.

As the sporadic fire flew overhead, Molembe pushed aside his pack and lay flat on his back, holding his Colt Commando across his chest. He looked over at Bolan. "Any ideas?"

"Two. We can play dead until they come looking for us, or we can take it to them."

"The problem with attacking is *this,*" the African replied, raising the Colt Commando. "Unless I get lucky, they're out of my effective range."

"They don't know that. You can lay down some covering fire, and I'll give them something to think about."

Molembe nodded. Like most of the other men pursuing the mercs, he carried the short-barreled Colt. Ideal for special-forces ops and in-close fighting, the weapon gave up a lot of accuracy past sixty yards.

The Desert Knight rear guard had taken position about three hundred yards away.

Bolan was equipped for in-fighting and for sniping. For shorter range he had his Beretta 93-R in a shoulder holster. He also carried an M-16-A2. With a five-hundred-yard range he could easily reach the riverbed, although every time he looked, the mercs were keeping out of sight.

He was prepared for that, too. The M-16 dual purpose weapon was fitted with an M-203 pump-action grenade launcher.

Bolan pumped the aluminum barrel of the launcher and locked in a 40 mm high-explosive round. "Okay, guy," he said, "let's do it."

The Zandesian tracker sprang to his left and opened up with the Colt Commando. He hosed the air with a full-auto spray, then dived behind shelter again.

The mercenary force reacted instantly, several of their rifles nosing out of the trenches.

Bolan had edged to the right of the rocky shield and sighted in on the riverbed, triggering the M-203 as soon as the mercs appeared.

Three seconds later the grenade struck the far side of the riverbank, ripping into rock and clay and sending a fiery torrent of high explosives onto the ambushers.

As the volcanic geyser showered the mercs, Bolan loaded another HE round and fired it to the right, where some of the thunderstruck mercenaries had moved. While they were still recovering from the first assault, the Executioner launched a smoke grenade that provided scattered wisps of cover.

He and Molembe double-timed it downhill, zig-zagging all the way before taking refuge behind another ridge of baked sand and stone.

The rest of Molembe's trackers converged from left and right onto the site, inching toward the riverbed behind whatever scarce cover they could find, firing staccato bursts at the Desert Knights.

Bolan alternated the 40 mm loads, firing heat, smoke and fragmentation grenades at the mercs' position.

The enemy force spread out, extending their firing line and sending steady streams of return fire at the Africans. But there weren't as many weapons firing this time.

Bolan guessed there were about a dozen or more left standing by now.

Though the trackers had fewer men for now, the tide had turned. The riverbed was a death trap. Enemy blood was flowing like water, and reinforcements were on the way.

The mercenaries couldn't attack the scattered forces of the trackers, nor could they abandon their position without getting picked off.

"We've got them," Bolan stated.

The security chief nodded. "Just have to pick up the pieces." He loaded another magazine into the hot-barreled Colt. He'd already run through several clips.

Now that they were within killing range, he'd fired with brutal effect, cutting down the defenders as they peered over the edge of their trenches. It was like tearing off the tops of picket fences, but the splinters were bone and blood.

Two of Molembe's trackers caught the scent of victory and let it carry them away. They raced straight toward the riverbed, firing full bore, not trying to evade enemy guns as they opened up on the mercs.

But the fight wasn't over yet.

At least not for the enemy forces, who concentrated their fire on the luckless duo.

The first volley ripped the lead man from head to toe and side to side, kicking him flat on his back, a lead-laden crucifix taking bloody shape on his desert camouflage uniform.

The second man realized his error and tried to dive for cover. But the snipers had his mark. He leaped right into a burst that riddled his face and punched him into the sand.

A tragic waste of life, Bolan thought. Some of the men were competent trackers but inexperienced warriors. Though the battle was almost over, the other side hadn't panicked, hadn't given up the fight.

They were hard-core, well picked by Fowler.

But the tide of battle had turned and would soon sweep the mercs away. It was only a question of time.

As the echoes of gunfire faded away and both sides paused to assess the damage, the sound of heavy rotors drummed the air.

The noise grew louder, closer, then the Lynx gunship appeared on the horizon. Painted with streaks of cloudy blue camouflage on the sides of the cabin, the utility war-horse hovered above a jagged ridge for a moment before dropping straight down out of sight.

The men on the ground looked toward the ridge, the trackers with enthusiasm, the defenders with dread.

"I hope that's *our* taxi," Bolan called to Molembe, who'd dropped behind a sandy promontory to establish contact with the choppers.

"It's Serpentine Force," the man replied, the handset dwarfed in his hand as he talked to the pilot.

"A force of one?"

Molembe shook his head and raised two fingers while he continued to talk with the pilot. He gestured to his left toward the ridge, where the chopper had disappeared, then the right, indicating a companion chopper en route.

The Zandesian nodded a few times as he spoke, shielding his eyes as he looked toward the ridge.

"He wants smoke," Molembe stated.

"He's got it."

The Executioner inched forward and to the right of the cover he'd chosen on the run. It was a clump of rock and clay about a foot and a half tall, capping a slight incline. Tall enough for a tombstone, the Executioner thought, if he showed too much silhouette. But the choppers needed to know where to concentrate their fire to finish off the resistance.

He pumped the M-203 to lock in the 40 mm load, then hugged the scorching sand and rock as he propped his elbow into the ground and fired a smoke grenade.

Seconds later smoke billowed from the riverbed trench, provoking a barrage of automatic fire that ripped into the sand and clay round Bolan's position. But it was a short-lived volley.

The chopper was making its move.

The Lynx came in from the left, firing two HE rockets. The first detonated in the bottom of the riverbed and sent a wall of flame and debris tearing into the defenders.

The second rocket exploded into the ground several feet to the left of the trench, bombarding the defenders with rocks and sheets of flame.

While smoke and flame shrouded the Desert Knights, the chopper came in for its strafing run, opening up with its 7.62 mm minigun. The solid line of lead cut down a quartet of the stunned mercs before they could even think about evasive maneuvers.

The sturdy Lynx followed the course of the riverbed, sustaining several hits that clanged into its armor-plating but caused little damage. It was a one-sided war, with the chopper returning fire a thousandfold.

Lead fell like sheets of rain until the Lynx finished its run and veered to the right to make way for the second chopper's attack.

It was hell times two.

A battery of 68 mm SNEB rockets flashed from the launcher of the second Lynx, bursting overhead as they neared the riverbed and unleashing a metal storm of antipersonnel steel darts over the survivors.

The chopper's machine guns opened up as it roared over the riverbed.

Bolan and the Zandesian trackers watched the pounding in silence. In a way it seemed like overkill, but this was war to the max. The mercs had shown no mercy for the legionnaire they'd used for target practice, and in turn they expected no mercy from Molembe's men.

Just the same, the Zandesian made the attempt, his basso voice sweeping over the gulf between them and calling for their surrender.

Several shots rang out, the few survivors firing in desperation. They wouldn't quit.

Molembe hand-signaled two of his men who carried drum-loaded automatic shotguns—Armsel Strikers, veritable cannons.

The Zandesian shotgunners split up as they approached the jagged riverbed and dropped in from both sides, the remaining trackers providing covering fire into the entrenched mercs.

A few moments later the Armsel Strikers roared, the 12-round drums of thunder emptying in less than three seconds.

The rest of the trackers swarmed toward the trench, jumping down into the dust, dirt and blood.

Crammed into a thin crevice, a bullet-riddled mercenary was screaming in his death throes. The first tracker to reach him fired one shot and freed him from his agony.

Two other shots echoed down the line as the Zandesians instinctively delivered coup shots to the dying mercs.

Then it was over.

Molembe called in the choppers while the rest of his men secured the landing zone, spreading out in case any more mercs were in the area, hiding.

But the rest of the Desert Knights were long gone.

In a stinging whirlpool of dirt and sand kicked up by the rotors, the helicopters landed.

While the first chopper ferried a handful of Molembe's men across the sand pan where they'd left their vehicles, Bolan stepped to the edge of the riverbed and looked down at the men who were sprawled out on the bottom.

The Zandesians methodically combed through the mercs' gear for weapons, ID, money, anything that might reveal how Fowler had recruited his troops.

About half of the men were native Zandesians, the other half imports Fowler had brought in from Europe.

Bolan looked toward the mountains, where the main body of the mercs had fled. Then he looked down at the rearguard who'd stayed behind—forever.

"Fowler chose well," Bolan commented. "If the rest of his men are like this, we're in for one hell of a battle."

Molembe nodded. "Some are better, some are worse. But he can always buy more. Even though we've shut down his bank accounts, he's got supporters in the city, hidden funds and a lot of people who owe him. They'll provide more hired guns." The tall Zandesian looked hard at Bolan. "This will go on until we take him out."

"That's why I'm here."

"That's what we've been told. I'll want to know more about that soon." The man's gaze slid to the bodies of his own men who'd fallen, then to the bodies of his countrymen sprawled out on the riverbed. "But civil wars and revolutions don't always go according to schedule."

"I'm here until the end," the Executioner promised.

"We'll see."

Bolan understood his skepticism. The fight had taken its toll and its time, holding up the pursuit long enough for the rest of the mercs to get away and dig themselves into the mountain fortresses.

"Let's see it up close," the Executioner suggested, heading for the second chopper.

2

Night fell quickly, bringing with it a sudden chill and wind that shrieked and tugged at the flickering camp fires set up by the Zandesian trackers. The men were spread out on a plateau that looked down on the surrounding cliffs, caves and passes that sliced through Mont Bataille.

The Zandesian Intelligence chief had selected the higher elevation as the base for the operation against the Desert Knights.

Serpentine Force helicopters had brought in fresh supplies and reinforcements, many of whom were now scanning the notches and ridges of the mountain through the thermal-imager scopes mounted on their sniper rifles.

Now and then one of them fired at the ghostly images that whisked across their night-vision screens for a brief instant before retreating into the shadows.

The Desert Knights returned the favor at odd intervals, their own lookouts firing rounds that whined off the cliff wall.

The shooting had no effect on either side, and most likely wouldn't produce any casualties during the night. It was just routine, designed to keep the other side on edge.

Between the psychological barrages many of the Zandesians snatched a couple of hours' sleep in their tents, knowing that at sunup they could be scaling down the mountainsides, digging out the mercs.

Bolan sat with his back against a contoured wall of rock, sipping a cup of harsh black coffee and looking up at the cloudy sky.

Around him spires of weathered rock stood like steeples from the majestic church of a long-ago Earth.

This was hallowed ground—the land of Zandesian prophets, the land of exodus. For thousands of years it had changed hands as the Zandesians warred against invaders, as well as their own tribesmen. But one thing remained constant: the gods were always in residence in the mountains. Chased here over the centuries as new religions came with the French, English and German, some of the old gods still prevailed.

And their names weren't forgotten by many Zandesians who called upon them from time to time.

Like Martin Molembe, Bolan thought.

Sitting less than ten feet away from him, the Zandesian had been quiet since the troops had settled in. Quiet but attentive, almost as if he were seeking counsel from the old tribal rulers of Zandesi.

Why not? Bolan thought. It was an eerie setting out here in the mountains. The night air seemed to carry with it the promise of death, imminent rainstorms of war that would soon sweep across the country. Unless he and Molembe contained Heinrich Fowler's Desert Knights, perhaps those storms would wash away the seeds of freedom so recently planted.

In such a deadly atmosphere a man could use all the help he got, whether it came from the old tribal gods or from a man called the Executioner.

Bolan found himself drifting into a state of half sleep, resting his body, relaxing his mind, but still aware of the sounds around him.

Now and then the scrabbling of running footsteps echoed from a distant ridge, followed by the shuffling of falling rock cascading over the steep edges. Then there'd be a long moment of silence until the rock clattered below, followed by the sudden volleys of rifle fire that slashed through the silence like a whip.

Molembe clapped his hands suddenly, focusing his attention on Bolan. "And now you, eh?"

"Now me?"

"There are things I must know if we're to fight this war to the finish."

Bolan set his tin cup beside him in the dirt and said, "Anything I can tell you, I will."

"I see." Molembe frowned. "And who decides what you can reveal?"

"Me. It depends on what you want to know."

"To start with, I want to know why you're here. From what I've heard of you and what I witnessed myself, you're a dangerous man to have around."

"Could be."

"Dangerous to whom, I wonder."

The byzantine maneuverings of Heinrich Fowler had left their mark throughout the military and Intelligence agencies of Zandesi. An accomplished player, Fowler had them all worried about spies and traitors.

"I'll tell you one thing," Bolan said. "If I was after you, you'd be dead and gone, and I'd be on my way home."

"Then why have you come here?" Molembe asked. He paused for a moment and looked around him as if he could pluck the answer from thin air. "To fight for people you don't even know out of some crazy sense of honor? No, I don't think so." The tall African shook his head for emphasis. "That can't be the answer."

Bolan shrugged, leaned back and braced himself against the rocky perch. "If you want to do the asking and the answering, that's fine with me," he said. "Let me know when you're finished."

"D'accord," Molembe replied, the ghost of a smile crossing his face. He nodded his head slowly, as if revelation was dawning up on him. "Tell me, Mr. Belasko. What's your price? And just as important, how much more would the other side have to pay to buy your loyalty?"

"I've got no price. I'd need a lot of money and little sense to jump into this situation."

"What is it, then?" the African demanded. "Excuse me if I don't sound convinced, but I understand you aren't quite attached to the U.S. government. Not officially. You're here because some of our American friends buy your services from time to time—"

"No one buys me," Bolan interrupted him. "It's more of a symbiotic relationship. Sometimes we fight the same fight, sometimes we go our own way."

"All the way to Zandesi."

"I'm here because a friend asked me to come. He thinks I should be here, and now that I see what's going on, I think so, too."

The Executioner thought back to the offshore briefing he'd had with Hal Brognola aboard one of four U.S. amphibious assault ships patrolling the Atlantic. Each vessel carried a Marine battalion and an assault helicopter squadron.

Carrying them was one thing. Using them was another.

The situation in Zandesi was a political minefield. If the U.S. went in with full strength, Fowler's people could brand them as imperialist warmongers and pull out all the stops in their guerrilla war, blaming the escalating violence on the U.S. presence.

Considering what had already happened, it would be a good propaganda ploy.

But at the moment the American warships were simply cruising offshore in international waters, making a show of potential force.

The real force was the Executioner.

Brognola's below-decks briefing had made it clear that for now Bolan could count on precious little overt support.

"What else is new?" Bolan had asked.

"For starters," the head Fed said, "my head's on the chopping block this time." He clasped his hands together and reflexively cracked his knuckles. Then, as if he could ward off the invisible, inevitable fall of a guillotine blade, he rubbed the back of his neck.

The man was under a lot of pressure this time, sweating both bullets and blood.

The personal threat to Hal Brognola caught Bolan's full attention. Aside from their years of friendship, the Justice man was an arm of Bolan's personal operations. A long arm. The big Fed was still a field man at heart, despite his rise in the covert bureaucracy. It was Brognola who kept the lions at bay so Bolan could have free rein, and who maintained the uneasy alliance between the Executioner and the U.S. government.

Their relationship was rock solid whether he was working for the Justice Department or not. Sometimes on his own missions Bolan needed to tap into Uncle Sam's covert apparatus. Brognola came through whenever he could, with few questions asked—just enough to know what to expect so he could prepare for the fallout.

Bolan paid back that trust time and again. Few questions asked.

This time was no different.

Brognola had stuck his neck out in Zandesi when the people had seized their chance to throw off the yoke of behind-the-scenes dictator Heinrich Fowler and his Zandesian front man, Emil Nashonge.

Representatives of the Free Election Party—FEP— had turned to the U.S. ambassador for guidance and for assistance. Among their leaders were several pro-American Zandesian officers who'd trained in the United States and were decidedly pro-Western. Chief among them was a military Intelligence officer named Martin Molembe.

Many of the officers had been sponsored by Hal Brognola a decade ago when the U.S. was in need of a friendly West African ally. Contacts were made, careers were pushed and the groundwork was laid.

But that was yesterday.

Times changed, perceptions changed.

With many Soviet operations winding down in Africa—as much due to bankruptcy as ideology—it no longer seemed so important to prop up a floundering West African nation. So when the FEP finally made its move to topple Nashonge's corrupt regime, the U.S. had to choose between lending a hand or turning its back.

The decision went against helping Zandesi.

The President's military and Intelligence advisers counseled against getting the United States mired in a long and bloody African conflict. In effect, they wanted the U.S. presence to melt, to pretend that Zandesi never existed.

But Brognola pulled every string he could. It wasn't in his nature to abandon friends. He called in favors from just about everyone he'd ever dealt with. And the tide turned when his circle of insiders went to bat for him.

The U.S. made a sudden about-face.

There was much talk of standing by old friends, of shoring up democracy at every chance. The U.S. called for UN observers and a peacekeeping force to ensure fair elections.

The movement spiraled, and an international body of statesmen and soldiers descended on Zandesi.

Everything went smoothly.

Until the election votes came in, ousting Emil Nashonge and turning the presidency over to Leopold Sabda, the FEP's choice.

That's when several UN observers were massacred, the small UN peacekeeping force was driven from the country and Leopold Sabda was taken prisoner by Heinrich Fowler and his embryonic democracy held hostage.

And now Zandesi was a few steps away from anarchy. Fowler's Desert Knights were ready to give it the final push.

It was up to Bolan and Martin Molembe to keep it from going over the edge.

Molembe's deep voice tugged Bolan back to the present. "That's your final answer?" the African asked. "You're risking your life because a friend asked you to?"

"Best reason that comes to mind."

"You place a high value on friendship."

"That's about all a man can count on these days," Bolan said. "And if it's good, it's about all a man needs. But it cuts both ways. Sometimes a friend will save your life . . . and sometimes he'll risk it."

"I'll keep that in mind."

3

Heinrich Fowler's callused left hand gripped the razor-sharp veins of rock running down the cliff side, balancing himself as he nimbly circuited the slender walkway that led to the cave outlet halfway down the cliff.

At times the trail was tightrope thin, passing beneath a series of handholds carved from the rock. But Fowler continued moving at the same pace, neither looking down nor back until he reached the mouth of the cave.

He stepped into the dark shadows and walked softly over the shifting path of pebbles and stone that served as a perimeter warning. No matter how skilled a man was, it was impossible to enter the cave without disturbing the splintery carpet of rock.

Cold, moist air coiled up from below as he moved deeper into the sloping cavern.

Like many of the caves that honeycombed the mountains, this one had several passages that gently sloped downward and some that plummeted straight down like a subterranean express to Hades.

As he moved along slowly and adjusted his eyes to the dimness, the musty smell of earth filled his nostrils. Despite his gloomy surroundings, Fowler carried himself as if he were still back in the marbled halls of the presidential palace, a mercenary maestro plucking the strings of Emil Nashonge's government.

He was dressed in desert fatigues. His jaw was clean-shaven, and his longish blond hair was neatly tied back with a thong like those of Germanic warriors of old, a Teutonic knight reborn and ready for battle.

Instead of sword and spear, he had a long-bladed commando knife sheathed at his side and a Skorpion machine pistol slung over his arm.

But he didn't need to rely on the weapons.

The notched short-sleeve shirt showed ribbons of vein and muscle. Despite the unlimited pleasures available to him back at the capital, he never let himself fade away. It was part family tradition, part necessity. Fowler had to stay in fighting form. That was the only thing that made the good things in life ready for the taking.

The Fowler clan had ruled behind the scenes in Zandesi for decades, and it hadn't been by accident or by chance. They ruled by force and fear. There was no other way. And though it was inevitable that there were times the clan was eclipsed by rival powers in Zandesi, the Fowlers always planned for a victorious return.

Which would be soon, he thought as he followed the steady descent of the cave floor.

Ten steps later he turned a sharp corner and came to a complete stop, staring straight ahead.

A short-barreled automatic rifle stared back at him, aimed right at his forehead.

"Morning, Fowler," the guard said, nodding his head and lowering his weapon. He wore shorts, a T-shirt and had a bandanna wrapped around his head. Round spectacles gave the lean mercenary a deceptively owlish look.

"Morning, Gauclere." Fowler glanced around the cave. "How's it going?"

"Slowly like always. But time passes. Soon I'll have my reward."

"A day at the beach?" Fowler asked. In his long shorts Gauclere almost looked like a lifeguard on one of Zandesi's beach resorts. A chill lingered in the air from the cold mountain night, but Fowler guessed the man wore such light garb to help him stay awake. The field jacket he'd worn during the night stood guard next to him, hanging from a stake like a scarecrow.

"The hell with a day at the beach," Gauclere growled. "A night back on the strip, now that's worth thinking about."

"You can have a month of such nights when we take back the capital. That I promise you."

The merc's eyes flashed brightly for a moment, but then his nonchalant gaze returned once again. A hard war awaited them first.

He leaned back against the hollowed-out side of the cave and rested his foot on a small rocky perch. He lighted a cigarette, then as an afterthought tilted the pack toward his superior.

Though Fowler preferred a pipe, he took one of the offered cigarettes and fired it up.

Despite Gauclere's casual manner—always a nod instead of a salute, always a familiar tone of address—he was one of the best soldiers Fowler had. Years of living under the African sun had made his skin bronzed, weathered and leathered. Years of soldering with Fowler had hardened his soul just the same.

Gauclere was much more than just a guard.

He was whatever Fowler needed. He'd demonstrated that time and again, most recently when one of the captured bodyguards became too much of a nuisance to Fowler.

It was Gauclere who staked him to the ground, Gauclere who commanded the firing squad.

Fowler finished his cigarette, then stubbed it out in the dirt at his feet. "Now tell me," he said. "How are our distinguished dignitaries?"

"They're alive." Gauclere shrugged. "Mostly."

"Any trouble?"

"Nothing unexpected. One of them tried to make a break for it a few hours ago and was taken care of."

Fowler nodded.

From the next chamber he could hear the other guards talking. He'd detailed enough men to handle Leopold Sabda's captive cabinet and defend the cave from attack. The escape attempt was prepared for as a matter of course. Men who thought they were condemned had little to lose.

Fowler spoke with his man a bit longer, discussing whether Sabda's people should be moved again.

Gauclere counseled against the move. "Too many of them, and too many risks. It doesn't pay to shepherd them around so much."

"On the contrary," Fowler said. "It pays quite well. At least for a man of your experience."

"Of course. Whatever you wish."

"I wish I was back in Zandeville," Fowler said. "In control again. Can you grant that wish, my friend?"

"I can follow your orders. Wherever that leads, I'll give you full credit—or blame. Rest assured, if it leads to my death instead of the capital I'll come back and haunt you."

Fowler laughed. "An admirable trait, but you're beginning to sound like a goddamn Zand. It's here and now that counts. And the only spook we have to fear is the American they've brought in."

Thanks to his man in Serpentine Force, who'd dropped his chopper down in the desert for a rendezvous, Fowler knew all about the pursuit—and the pursuer.

"What's his name?" Gauclere asked.

"His cover name is Michael Belasko, but I'd say it's an alias. Regardless, he'll die just as easy as any man if he gets into our gun sights."

Fowler dropped his hand onto the merc's shoulder. "And don't worry about logistics for the prisoners. Perhaps there won't be as many of them by the time we're ready to move."

Fowler headed for the next chamber, walking past a mixed force of European hardguys and Zandesian loyalists who were sipping tea and water. A few of them who were obviously drinking something stronger discreetly moved their tin cups out of his view.

He knew the drinkers among them and knew how to deal with them. They were controllable drunks who kept themselves on a steady keel. No critical missions or covert ops for those soldiers. But these men of the grape and wards of whiskey had their uses, carrying their courage around with them so they'd stand firm during battle.

The important thing was that they were loyal—loyal to his payroll and allergic to the law like most of the Desert Knights.

By and large the Zandesians fighting for him were the ones who'd be hanged by their countrymen for crimes and atrocities committed during Nashonge's reign.

Fowler continued moving downward, walking the same path as exiled kings had done a millennium ago. It was no accident that the Desert Knights had fled to Mont Bataille.

It wasn't just a haphazard flight into the desert. He'd planned for his stay in the rocky fortress long ago. Fowler had known that revolt against Nashonge's rule was inevitable, and he'd prepared well for the occasion.

Caches of weapons and food had been flown out to the fortress of rock. Caves had been widened and their courses altered, like stone-banked rivers drifting throughout the canyons and ridges of the mountain.

Hillside crevices were shielded with natural-looking rock formations to provide hiding places, as well as sniper positions for the desert mercs.

Fowler had selected several outposts for his outcast army, zigzagging up and down the canyons. He'd also established a line of battle through which he'd lead the enemy stage by stage until they besieged Mont Bataille—an impossible task.

And while the enemy forces were tied up in the mountains, Fowler would strike back at the capital and take back what was his.

The rule of Zandesi.

PRESIDENT ELECT Leopold Sabda looked over the members of his cabinet, sprawled in battered heaps throughout the wide, high-roofed cavern.

Like him they were thirsty. Their lips were parched, their stamina sapped. They were given just enough water and food to maintain life.

Tattered suits hung on the beaten frames of the men, illustrious scarecrows who were testament to what happened to those who defied Heinrich Fowler.

The one woman among them was also dressed in rags. She was the wife of one of Sabda's wealthier backers, but now she looked like someone who lived in the streets. Her dress was torn in several places, as was her soul. Every time the guards entered their chamber she cringed, as if imagining what horror was in store for her.

There was little that Leopold Sabda could do for her. Or for any of them.

Except perhaps to die well.

He choked back the tears and the anger. The others had practically stopped listening to him. Blank gazes met his eyes when he spoke to them. Or sometimes they looked away, worn down by his unfounded optimism.

Sabda had almost stopped listening to his inner voice, which said they'd somehow survive this ordeal, that *he* could get them out alive.

It was hopeless. His small band was beaten. They were scattered around the spiny contours of the cave, huddled in small pitiful pockets. Withdrawn from one another, withdrawn from him.

Their leader had led them into despair.

His first official act as president of Zandesi was to be captured, to bear mute witness to the slaughter of his people as Fowler's gunmen mercilessly cut down anyone in their way. Like cattle—no, like sheep—they'd been herded from the speaker's platform in Capital Square during Sabda's first address to the Zandesian people.

He'd been cut off in midspeech by a volley of automatic gunfire that scythed through the crowd, the first of many as Fowler's men began firing from every direction. Then came the blood, the screams and the chaos, the indiscriminate slaughter that had led to his capture.

The slaughter hadn't ended there.

Fowler had demonstrated how tenuous their hold on life was while they were under his control. The trek to Mont Bataille had taken its toll, leaving more of Sabda's followers dead in the sand. Most of the presidential bodyguards had been killed in the early stages of captivity.

A future they all shared, he thought. They were all under death sentence.

The cabinet members spent their time sleeping, hatching improbable escape attempts or, in the case of his defense minister, Stephen Ward, mumbling and ranting.

At the moment Ward sat some twenty feet away from him, first looking his way, then looking wildly around the cavern as if his tormentors were hiding in the crevices.

He was delirious, half-dead. He was covered with bruises, his eyes were nearly swollen shut and his broken ribs made breathing an absolute agony.

This human wreckage had made a bid for escape during the night, attacking one of the guards while he'd been making his rounds.

Almost as if it had been rehearsed, the guard turned at the sound of his rapid approach and caved in the side of his face with his rifle butt. Teeth cracked and cheekbone imploded, blood sluiced from his mouth and he dropped to the dusty floor like stone. Then the guard casually kicked Ward's ribs in while the other guards who had poured into the room kept Sabda and the others at bay.

It wasn't the first time they'd battered Ward.

Ever since their exodus began, the guards had arbitrarily chosen Ward as the butt of their brutality. Any time the prisoners committed an infraction, Ward was the one who was punished. He was beaten and mocked until the fear and rage had driven him out of his mind. And though the treatment seemed irrational, it was a very calculated terror that drove a wedge between Ward and the other prisoners.

The constant mistreatment made Sabda look even more ineffectual in the eyes of his cabinet, and it made him a pariah in the puffed and closed eyes of Ward. "Don't come," Ward was saying now. "Don't come...I'm not ready." It was like a chant, a page from the *Book of the Dead*. The defense minister trembled, groaned in pain, then descended into a drone of incoherence.

There was nothing more Sabda could do for him. He'd demanded medicine for the man and had been refused. The countless times he'd tried to go to him had only made Ward hysterical. Now Ward's state of mind and weakened body matched each other in the rate of their decline.

Sabda heard voices in the gallery outside. A few moments later Heinrich Fowler bowed his head and stepped through the entrance.

The mercenary captain looked fresh, happy, as if he were attending a social function rather than step-ping into a dungeon.

"Mr. President," Fowler said, his voice echoing in the room as he approached.

"What is it?"

"Please stand so we can talk as equals." He spoke in measured, formal English, the language in which all were fluent.

When Sabda got to his feet, it was apparent that they were hardly equals. The mercenary had several inches on him and had an impressive physical bulk. Sabda's strength was mainly intellectual, and at the moment even that was in doubt.

He felt the eyes of his people upon him, and from the corner of his eye he saw the defense minister freeze, not daring to move an inch while the predatory mercenary was about.

"What is it, Fowler?" Sabda repeated. "What do you want?"

"I want a bipartisan government. You and I working together to prevent a civil war and restore law and order to the country."

Sabda laughed. "Like the law and order you've established here?" He gestured around the cave, pointing out the sorry condition of the other prisoners.

Fowler gave them a cursory glance. "If you're really concerned about their plight, perhaps it's time you joined me in hammering out an agreement."

"We can hammer out nothing."

"I see." The mercenary leader reached into his pocket and removed a slim voice-activated tape recorder. "Would you care to say that for the benefit of the Zandesian people? I plan on issuing a statement on my position—I think the people would like to hear yours."

He held out the recorder. "Is there anything you wish to say?"

Sabda kept silent.

Fowler nodded. "Yes, this often happens in the early stages of negotiation. One side doubts the other's sincerity. Let me show you how sincere I can be."

He spun around and stalked across the dusty cavern floor toward the fallen minister. Ward pushed himself away from the crevice in a desperate lunge, but Fowler hurtled in front of him and sweep-kicked him off his feet.

At the same time he unholstered his Skorpion machine pistol, pointed it at Ward's head and fired a burst, the jackhammer slugs echoing in the confines of the cave.

Ward collapsed, face forward.

The rest of Sabda's people moved forward as if they were going to rush the merc. But they stopped, frozen in place, aware that they were no match for the man even if he didn't have the gun, let alone the guards who were already on their way.

And then they gasped.

The defense minister came back from the dead. The dazed man pushed himself up onto his hands and stared at the bullet holes studding the ground in front of him.

"My aim gets better each time," Fowler stated, glancing at Sabda. He held the machine pistol aloft. "What do you think? Shall I try again?"

"No."

"Excellent decision," Fowler replied in a casual tone as he walked away from the man who'd just been granted a stay of execution. "Very presidential. Now we can work on a message together. I want you to say something like 'in the interest of democracy, I'm going to establish a bipartisan government with Heinrich Fowler and his party.'"

"That's impossible!"

"I understand," Fowler said. "You're a man of conscience. So am I. We both must do what we think best for the country." He headed back toward Ward and lowered the Skorpion until the barrel touched his forehead. "There will be no missing this time."

"Stop!" Sabda shouted. "Stop this madness. I'll talk to the people."

Like a reporter who'd just snared a rare interview, Fowler hurried over to Sabda and once again held out the minirecorder. "Very good, Mr. President. But before you speak, remember one thing. Don't cross me in any manner. Say nothing that might alert anyone to my whereabouts. After all, we need each other. I can't rule without you, and you can't live without me. But the others..." He looked at the cabinet members.

They tried to stare back impassively, but all looked as if they were calculating how soon a rope would drop around their necks.

The room was dead quiet, as if a spell had been cast. The magician stood there calmly smiling at them like a friend, their only friend in the world who wished them well but might be forced to kill them if Sabda didn't cooperate.

"They're disposable," Fowler continued. "How long they live depends on what you say."

"As you wish."

"Let us begin."

Fowler handed the recorder to Sabda, and the imprisoned politician began his second public act, a traitorous speech.

"This is President Leopold Sabda," he began. "I'm in good health, and I'm speaking of my own free will. Our situation is dangerous, but no more dangerous than that of our country. We're all at risk. That's why I'm holding discussions with Heinrich Fowler...."

Sabda kept on talking in a calm manner, determined not to risk Fowler's wrath. He was under no illusions that he'd save the people in the room. Despite Fowler's manner, he knew they were condemned to die. All he'd done was to postpone their deaths for a while—and perhaps the death of Zandesi.

4

Ten miles east of Mont Bataille the shadow of a Lynx scout helicopter flew across the desert, a high-tech hawk with electronic talons readying for the kill.

The mast-mounted sight of the scout gave the pilot the luxury of zeroing in on the target without having to unmask his presence. Shielded by the moat of foothills surrounding the enemy outpost, the raised mast of the Lynx towered above the rotors and kept it safely out of sight.

The pilot locked his laser sight onto a Stonehenge-like formation of rock looming out of the desert. Huge slabs of rock were propped up against one another, some of them supporting oddly angled stone caps that looked like huge sundials and sacrificial altars. They were the ruins of a Zandesian kingdom that had flourished in this place thousands of years ago. Picked clean by time and archaeological plunderers, there was little left but barren rock.

And Desert Knights.

Less than fifteen minutes had passed since the scout radioed the Serpentine attack force that it had located a column of mercenaries who'd taken shelter at the crumbling redoubt.

Three fast-moving attack helicopters from Serpentine Force droned above the desert, staying low as they neared the scout chopper.

Mack Bolan rode in the lead aircraft, sitting in the staggered seat behind the copilot, his M-16 draped over his lap. He glanced out the window at the desert below, a granite-and-sand map of hills, ridges and long flat sand pans. There was little down there a man could live on, but plenty he could die from.

In the cabin behind him crouched a dozen desert commandos with weapons at the ready. They were silent, caught in the trance brought on by the rhythmic shuddering of the sun-baked metal cocoon and the knowledge that soon they'd be in the middle of a firefight.

There would definitely be an engagement, Bolan thought. From the scout aircraft's earlier report it sounded as if the enemy column was large enough to represent a breakout group from Fowler's main force. No civilians or captives were seen, just a group of hardmen who'd fired on the scout ship before the pilot dropped out of sight.

And Serpentine Force was drawn to them like a magnet. Perhaps drawn a bit too fast, the warrior thought. Before they'd lifted off, Bolan had had a hurried conversation with Martin Molembe about the sudden sighting that diverted them from their patrols in the honeycombed rock fortresses of Mont Bataille.

Something was a bit off, something that bothered the Executioner. Fowler was reputed to be a good military mind, and by and large his men were supposed to be seasoned pros. So why were they showing themselves while a helicopter was flying a recon of the area? It was either coincidence or something a lot more disconcerting.

Molembe recognized the situation as a possible setup, but at the same time he felt the troops needed a victory to rouse public attention back in the capital.

If it was a trap, they were going to spring it.

And they were going to do it full force.

Two other attack helicopters flanked them, slightly behind. They were similarly armed, carrying Hellfire missiles, rockets and grenades and a squad of commandos handpicked by Molembe.

By now Bolan was familiar with most of the faces and names. He knew the core group that Molembe depended upon, the men the Zandesian security chief trusted with his life. Soon Bolan would be doing the same.

The lead chopper nosed above the circular lip of rock and established visual contact with the scout.

"Target hand-over." The static-tinged voice of the scout pilot brought an immediate response from the lead attack chopper. The pilot drifted above the ridge again, then fired a Hellfire missile.

Homed on the target via the laser receiver in the nose of the missile, the Hellfire streaked toward the stone formation, an arrow tail of the fire marking its path.

The armor-piercing warhead struck the rock, detonating in a cloud of smoke and fire.

Seconds later another missile blasted into the same area.

Antipersonnel rockets flew toward the target area when the second attack chopper made its pass, then raked the brimstone clouds settling upon the ruins with five hundred rounds of machine-gun fire.

The third Lynx provided backup, unloading a barrage of suppressive fire any time Fowler's troops showed themselves and attempted to return fire. The chopper's machine gun and grenade launchers knocked them into oblivion.

In deadly choreography the assault aircraft droned in toward the target, unleashing explosive strikes and suppressive fire. Warheads rocked the enemy position, followed up by the steady chatter of miniguns.

The steady pounding took a deadly toll.

Groaning rock walls and capstones collapsed under the barrage, tumbling downhill to reveal a series of dugout tunnels and fortified trenches that had been hidden by the now-uprooted dolmens.

Like taking the cap off an anthill, Bolan thought as the helicopter he rode in flew by the stronghold for another pass. Men sprinted downhill from the shattered shelter, firing wildly toward the choppers, but for the most part looking to get out of the trap they'd dug themselves in.

With the same single-minded fury, the helicopters poured their fire into the redoubt, the explosive charges eroding man and mountain alike in a thunderous barrage while the scout chopper circled the area in search of more pockets of Fowler's hardmen.

Then the attack choppers swooped down over the uneven terrain to drop off the commandos.

Too rocky to land the aircraft, the drop-off point was a moonscape of jagged spires and depressions with a protective ridge that kept them out of the line of fire.

In a matter of seconds the commandos slid down to the ground on nylon ropes that hung like tendrils from the helicopter.

The moment the Executioner touched down, he moved away from the drop-off point. Behind him he heard the grunts and footfalls of several more commandos as they hit the ground.

The wasplike shadows of the Lynxes blocked out the harsh sun for a few moments, then dwindled rapidly as the helicopters began to circle the outer perimeter of the redoubt like heavy metal carrion.

They'd softened up the enemy. Now it was up to the commandos to finish the attack. From here on in it would be up close and personal.

Bolan ran uphill in a crouch. After a quick scan of the smoke and thunder that marked the position of the Desert Knights, he crested the ridge, bearing down on them with the grenade launcher up and ready. He thumped a round of smoke into their midst, adding to the chaos and providing cover for the attack.

Heartbeats later he sprinted straight for the ruins, clambering over the huge slabs of rock that were now scattered over the ground like toppled tombstones.

To his left he spotted the broad-shouldered figure of Martin Molembe leading a squad of his men. He was standing on a slanting rock, gesturing his troops forward while he triggered a burst of fire from the Colt Commando.

Enemy fire blindly met the attack.

Bursts of flame punctuated the smoke and sent a hail of lead clanking down on the rocks at the Executioner's feet, sending him airborne for a moment as he jagged to his right.

The warrior whipped the M-16 from left to right, triggering a full-auto burst toward the sputtering flashes of enemy fire. The return fire dropped off quickly.

Molembe's commandos followed suit as they climbed the rock-strewn ascent, now and then dropping behind cover to fire their weapons uphill.

As Bolan neared the lip of the shattered rampart, a mercenary threw down his rifle and raised his hands overhead. "Don't shoot," he pleaded. "Don't shoot."

"Don't move," Bolan ordered.

The man nodded. He looked like a shell-shocked survivor of a nuclear blast. His bald head was red and bleeding, and the fringe of hair on the sides of his head was singed. His clothes were torn, and his body was bleeding from several small wounds.

The man's cry of surrender was contagious, echoing up and down the line of Desert Knights who found themselves looking up into the smoking barrels of automatic rifles.

Bolan held his fire, rapidly scanning the line for movement.

The surrender had taken the Desert Knights as much by surprise as it had the commandos who'd stormed their position.

But it wasn't quite a total surrender.

To the left of the first man who'd surrendered, Bolan saw a bearded and bloodied hardguy who was gradually coming out of his kneeling position, the pistol in his right hand slowly inching forward.

The man wanted to go out in a blaze of glory.

Bolan snap-fired from his hip, catching the gunner square in the chest. Blood sieved from the merc's darkened uniform as he dropped to the ground, the pistol flying from his hand.

It was a dangerous moment.

Was the surrender in effect or not? The thought passed like lightning through the minds of the defenders. In the uncertainty there was always the danger that the opposition might make a grab for their weapons. Molembe's people might decide to solve the problem the hard way and unload on the would-be prisoners.

But then Martin Molembe's voice suddenly bellowed down the line. Like a command from Moses on the mountain, he ordered all of the mercenaries to drop facedown onto the ground.

When all heads turned his way, he continued in a clear and low voice, "Anyone still standing will be shot."

Like a stack of soft dominoes falling, the Desert Knights sprawled out on the ground.

Molembe's men jumped down into the clay-bottomed trench and separated the weaponry from their enemy before they could think twice about their decision. The Zandesian troopers rattled off information about weapons, food caches and the presence of other Desert Knights in the area. According to the hardmen, their group was the entire force.

They were carefully herded away from the redoubt into the harsh sunlight.

"So much for their trap," Molembe said when he drifted over toward Bolan. The big Zandesian wasn't gloating. He was eager to claim a victory.

"Yeah," Bolan said. "We got some live ones this time." He glanced at the prisoners filing away from the shattered cliff-side fortress under their heavy guard. They were a mixture of Zandesians and Europeans, most of them hardly looking like so-called Desert Knights. More like serfs sent to war by a medieval baron.

The Zandesian Intelligence chief caught the skepticism in Bolan's voice. "Yes," he said, "we have a small victory. We have prisoners, and we have casualties on our side. What is wrong with that? Unless, of course, you are a *malade imaginaire.*"

"No," Bolan replied, "I'm not looking to see the worst. I'm just trying to see the facts."

"The facts are right there." Molembe pointed toward the mercenaries who'd never leave their positions, the dead bodies arranged in strange heaps that sported grimaces and looks of surprise, the last vestiges of life before their souls left them behind.

"Yeah, that's part of it," Bolan agreed. While the prisoners were led downhill, the Executioner kept glancing around him, as if he expected to see more resistance.

Overhead the helicopters reconned the rest of the circular redoubt, covering the terrain sector by sector. Molembe kept in contact with them by a thin headset and mike. "The scout chopper's been directing the others," he said. "We've got an all clear from him."

"Yeah, but I've got a feeling it's not."

Molembe nodded. Sweat appeared on his forehead, then dried quickly from the warm winds that drifted up from the desert flats. "We can't run an operation just on your feelings alone."

"How about yours?"

"Without doubt," Molembe replied, "I share your sentiments. But I don't know why."

"It's the same kind of feeling you get when you find out you're walking in the middle of a minefield," Bolan said. "From here on in, each step we take could be our last."

As if they were doing just that, Molembe's commandos carefully scoured the area as they climbed the face of rock that had shielded the Desert Knights.

The area in front of them was secure and there was still no sign of anything amiss, but the gnawing sensation wouldn't go away.

"Take a good look at them," Bolan directed, gesturing toward the dozen or so survivors who'd been herded off to a small gully by Molembe's guards.

The security chief looked over at where the prisoners sat cross-legged with their hands folded on top of their heads. "What about them?"

"They were too green. Almost as if they'd been dropped here for the express purpose of being annihilated."

"I've considered that," Molembe said. "But if it was a ruse, where's the payoff?"

The answer came in the form of a loud explosion on the far side of the redoubt where a broad spear of rock jutted out into the surrounding flatland.

A Stinger missile had streaked across the sky, homing in on the attack helicopter Bolan had been riding earlier. Shards of metal imploded from the blast, opening the side of the helicopter like a tin can.

The chopper rocked and shuddered, engines sputtering as if turned in midair, and tried to make it back to safety.

It didn't.

A second ground-launched Stinger exploded on the pilot's side of the aircraft, blowing out the glass and the pilot all at once.

The chopper spiraled in an awkward corkscrew pattern before smashing into the ground, pieces of metal flying across the desert floor like confetti.

Both remaining Lynxes headed straight for the downed chopper.

At the same time more than a score of armed figures appeared at the base of the rocks and opened up with heavy machine guns at the helicopters while a handful of men zeroed in on them and launched more missiles.

Both choppers fired flare and chaff dispensers to distract the missiles, flooding the sky with strips of radar-reflective chaff and hot-burning flares. As the aircraft drew back, they fired several strings of anti-personnel rockets at their attackers on the ground.

After the rockets burst in the air and needled with deadly metal spikes the Desert Knights who hadn't found cover, another wave of mercenaries wearing desert camouflage fatigues emerged from the rocks.

It was as if an entire army had lain in wait for the express purpose of downing the helicopters. That was Fowler's main target. If the Zandesi Air Force was knocked out of action, Fowler's main body of hardmen would be that much harder to dig out.

Molembe trained his binoculars on the right flank where the mercenaries were spreading out. They moved with split-second timing, taking cover as they swarmed over the rocky terrain and set up wellfortified positions for their Stinger-carrying squads. The entire side of the mountain had suddenly become a well-armed fortress.

The Desert Knights moved with such precision that it seemed as if they'd known every square inch of ground, as if it had all been carefully rehearsed.

"Where the hell did they come from?" Molembe asked.

"Ask the pilot in the scout chopper," Bolan grunted. "Wasn't he the one who swept that area?"

"He gave the all clear," Martin said, his voice low and somber, like a judge who'd just issued a death sentence.

"It looks like we've found Fowler's real fighters this time."

"Or maybe they found us." Molembe directed a half dozen of his men forward to set up a line of fire and slow the enemy's advance.

While the commandos prepared to deal with the new force of Desert Knights, Bolan studied the prisoners again. They seemed just as surprised as Molembe's people were to find so many mercenaries joining the action.

Almost all of them seemed surprised, Bolan realized. His eyes came to rest on a bushy-sideburned man who looked like an Aussie cowboy in a broad-brimmed hat that shaded his eyes. He watched the mercs calmly, as if he were aware of their presence and their ability—like a director who'd helped choreograph the play a dozen times already.

He had the aura of a man who thought he wouldn't be a prisoner long.

Maybe he wouldn't, Bolan thought. When this was over, he and the cowboy were going to have a long talk.

But right now they had to deal with the Desert Knights.

The choppers had pulled back and set down on the desert floor safely out of range. While the chopper crews reloaded the launchers with missiles they'd carried in the cabins, Molembe's troops were going to move against the Desert Knights to see how many of the missile-carrying mercs they could knock out before the helicopters came back.

"Which way you going to hit them?" Bolan asked, approaching Molembe after the Zandesian had conferred with a trio of his scouts.

"Over there," the man replied, pointing to a rise that offered a jagged wall of protection and at the same time gave his commandos a clear range of fire.

"Looks good," Bolan commented, studying the terrain. "Judging from the way things have been going, it looks too good." There was lots of protection, but at the same time, it offered a lot of potential traps. "If we go there, be prepared to find a few mercs underfoot."

"Think we'll find snakes under those rocks?"

"Snake eaters, maybe. If Fowler has special-forces types working for him, they could be dug in there and we wouldn't know it until we walked right in the middle of them."

"*If* they took the time to do it," Molembe stated. "But that would mean they've been setting this up for days now and we've been dancing to their tune."

"That sounds like the Fowler I was briefed on," Bolan said, remembering some of the merc's operations contained in his dossier.

"Yeah, it does," Molembe conceded. "If he could help it, he never left anything to chance. Nodding toward the rise again, he said, "Maybe that's the mine-field you were talking about before. A human one."

"We'll find out soon enough."

The African signaled the rest of his men, gave them a quick briefing and then moved toward the rise.

THE ZANDESIAN COMMANDOS crept over the sand-colored rise slowly, the barrels of their automatic weapons nosing every square inch, probing the shadows behind rock formations and lingering over the scattered rocks that lay in their path.

Many of the rock piles were large enough to conceal a man.

The body of commandos grew considerably smaller as they moved farther uphill. At several stages along the way, Molembe's men dropped back to cover suspicious-looking areas.

Bolan was halfway up the rise when the first of the enemy showed.

It was almost an imperceptible movement. A lid of what looked like solid rock was actually broken into two separate pieces, almost like a window. The uppermost section of rock tilted back, and the snout of a rifle poked out.

The Executioner spun to his right, instinctively homing the M-16 in on the small opening. He squeezed the trigger and hammered away at the gunman's perch.

There was a short cry of pain, and then like a jack-in-the-box, the man's spastic motion knocked over the top section of rock. He tumbled out, an uneven line of red bullet holes blossoming across the white-robed warrior, marking where he'd been struck.

At that first burst of gunfire the hill came alive.

Rocks toppled free and rifle barrels nosed out into the open as the hidden gunmen prepared to slaughter the Zandesians. But instead, the ambushers found themselves at the wrong end of a shooting gallery.

Zandesian commandos opened up on the ambushers with everything they had, strafing their hiding places with automatic fire, grenades and flamethrowers.

The commandos had carefully set up their own positions, zigzagging a string of three-man teams up the rise so they could cover all directions.

They didn't take any chances, unloading on all of the sites they'd previously picked out as possible hiding places.

Smoke and cordite clouded the rise, adding a ghostly backdrop to the bloody stage the panicked ambushers suddenly found themselves upon. Their role as shock troops had been changed at the last moment.

Now they were quickly becoming corpses.

Crumbling rock cascaded down the rise as death cries echoed from their shallow caves and old weapons dropped at their feet.

A burning gunman fled down the hill, his robes torched by the flamethrower. As the fiery tendrils chased after him, his robes consumed, a Zandesian commando fired a single mercy shot that silenced his scream and punched him to the ground.

One after the other the gunmen were forced from their ambush positions. Staying in their dugout positions while grenades and rifle fire blasted away at them was the same as committing suicide.

Several gunners came out firing and ran into a wall of lead. The others tossed their weapons out first, following with their hands up.

Soon only a handful of "ambushers" were left alive.

A Zandesian rifle team herded the survivors into a small circle where they stood quietly awaiting their fate.

While Molembe stayed behind to deal with the captives, he sent his subordinate officers forward to secure the rise and position snipers to greet the rest of the Desert Knights.

The long robes, headdresses and their light tawny complexions identified the new captives as Maskarai, desert tribesmen who'd long stayed out of the affairs of the warring Zandesian factions.

But the war had come to their territory and they'd chosen sides. For this group of tribesmen it was obviously the wrong side.

Molembe approached the tribesman who looked to be in command. He was the tallest and the calmest. His gray brows came to a sharp peak like small lightning bolts, and his eyes were equally fierce.

The bronzed Maskarai warrior wore the look of a man who had conquered death long ago and had accepted it as part of his calling. The only question that remained was the manner of his passing.

"Tell me your name," Molembe demanded.

The man considered, then responded in a proud voice. "I am called Zhoave," he said.

The name obviously struck a chord with Molembe's men, many of them shifting their stance for a better look at the desert chieftain.

And it also had plenty of currency with the security chief, who raised his eyebrows and stepped closer to the man. "I've heard that name often," he said. "Enough to be surprised that you and your men travel with Fowler's people."

"There was little choice in the matter," Zhoave replied. "We only want to live our own lives freely.

When the German told us of your plans, we decided to help him stop you."

"What plans?"

"To lay waste to the desert. To poison the wells and the waters and make sure no one could live out here. To kill everything in your path." He recited the parade of atrocities like a mantra that had been repeated to him several times over.

"What we do depends on the path we must take and the path chosen by others," Molembe told him. "If you choose to fight us, we can't walk away. But we never planned on destroying the desert as you claim. Such things are the province of Heinrich Fowler."

Zhoave folded his arms in front of him. "Four of our families were massacred by your soldiers—"

"It wasn't us. Perhaps you should look closer to home for the killers."

"You're saying the German would kill some of our own people just to enlist us against you?"

"He believes in tactics," Molembe replied, "not people."

"It could be so," the nomad admitted. "But who can we believe in time of war?"

"You can believe me. Our fight isn't with you, but with Fowler. Tell us what we wish to know and you're free to go."

"It's a trick," one of the Maskarai warriors warned.

"If it is," Zhoave said, "then it's one more jest before we die. Ask what you will. We have no reason to lie. The truth is very simple. We will fight who we must to remain free."

One by one the Maskarai tribesmen were separated from the others for questioning.

Their stories coincided. The Maskarai and the main body of Desert Knights had been there well in advance, digging themselves in and waiting for the Zandesians to be drawn there. There were no civilians or hostages kept by the mercs.

The smaller group of Desert Knights who now shared captivity with the tribesmen had no idea about the presence of another body of well-armed mercs. Like sacrificial lambs, the smaller group of mercenaries had been used as a snare to bring in Molembe's people.

Then the Maskarai tribesmen and the rest of the Desert Knights would down the helicopters and destroy the strike force.

The Maskarai were out of it for now, but the rest of the Desert Knights were still in good position. They controlled the area to the right and were slowly closing in on the Zandesian strike force. With their superior numbers they could either eliminate them by attrition or kill two birds at once and knock out the choppers when they came to airlift the commandos.

After the interrogation was over, two of Molembe's men gathered the weapons of the prisoners, unloaded them and then dropped them at their feet.

It was a random collection of semiautomatic MAS 1949 rifles, M-1 Garands and U.S. M-1 carbines that were postwar standard issue in the French army, rifles that inevitably made their way throughout the African colonies.

"You're free to go," Molembe said to the leader of the tribesmen. "As long as you go that way," he added, pointing back down the way they'd come.

Zhoave spoke quickly to his men, then bowed slightly to the tall Zandesian. The tribesmen picked up their weapons and under the eyes of a wary escort went back down the hill, away from the war.

While some of the security force grumbled about the release of the tribesmen, most of them went along with their superior's decision.

"Nice gambit," Bolan said as he watched the tribesmen depart.

Molembe shrugged. "If they come back to fight us, it's only a few more soldiers we face. But if they spread the word among their people . . . that might be one less army we have to fight."

"What about that army?" Bolan asked, gesturing toward the Desert Knights.

"They wanted to take on our air force. Soon their wish will be granted. If we can hold out that long."

THE STEADY DRONE of Spectre gunships and two resurrected German bombers of World War II vintage grew louder as they flew low across the Harana Desert. There were only five aircraft that were serviceable, five crews that could be trusted to carry out the attack.

By the time the Zandesi Air Force reached the stronghold of the Desert Knights, the mercenaries had formed a half circle around the rise.

Soon they'd overwhelm it.

But the Zandesian strike force was no longer there. It had withdrawn slowly, filing toward the desert lowlands. Only a small group remained on the rise, making a lot of noise and marking the enemy position with smoke and flares.

They, too, pulled back suddenly, scrambling down the rise as the planes streaked across the sky.

The first Spectre swooped low and opened up with 20 mm Vulcan cannons, chewing up the granite formations that hid the Desert Knights.

While lead rain poured down on the mercenaries' position, the two attack choppers flew into position for a follow-up run, launching their last missiles in an explosive volley that thundered across the mountain.

Two other gunships roared past the enemy, firing 105 mm howitzers. The armor-piercing blasts punched holes in the cliff sides, sending an avalanche of rock down upon the defenders.

While the Desert Knights were stunned by the explosions, the bombers made their runs, slowly flying overhead and dropping a string of CBU-55 cluster bombs. The one-hundred-pound canisters drifted toward the Desert Knights on parachutes, a gentle drop with a hellish payoff.

Bursting open on impact, the canisters spread clouds of ethylene oxide up and down the enemy position. Then the detonators went off, and the clouds ignited with an earth-shuddering blast.

With a blast effect of hundreds of pounds of pressure per square inch, the death cloud shredded every living thing it had settled on, practically obliterating the entire force of mercenaries.

Only a few dazed hardmen stumbled out of the rubble, firing their weapons in every direction.

Their gunfire came to an abrupt halt when they walked right into the line of automatic fire laid down by the returning Zandesian scouts.

And then a stillness fell over the desert as the Zandesian commandos saw up close what had happened to the foreign mercenaries and their own countrymen.

Civil war had happened, courtesy of Heinrich Fowler.

5

Zandeville, the capital of Zandesi, sprawled for miles, with open-air markets and shops standing in the shadows of modern office buildings. Small, thatched-roof houses and seaside villas zigzagged along the coastline, blending traditional with modern.

A bright jangling string of nightclubs and hotels flanked the coves and beaches.

Zandeville had returned to an uneasy normalcy since the inaugural massacre. Life went on.

During the day it was business as usual. Factories and farms outside the city proper were still operational, and in the city itself the usual horde of street vendors plied their goods.

But at night a carnival atmosphere settled over the clubs and seaside bars, almost as if the people were forcing themselves to have fun, to spend their money while they could. Beneath the sense of normalcy was the attitude that something was going to happen soon.

It was only a matter of time before one of the would-be rulers of Zandesi took control.

In the meantime the Zandesi Intelligence Service had assumed the dual role of police and defense force. Like the majority of the people, most members of ZIS supported the newly elected presidency of Leopold Sabda. This gave the ZIS officers a legitimacy in the eyes of the people.

And with the initial victories of Martin Molembe's troops against the Desert Knights, it gave the leader of the ZIS an equally solid currency with the people, convincing them they'd made the right choice in trusting him to caretake the government until the crisis was solved.

One of Molembe's first acts had been to attach former army personnel to police units in the street to maintain order and to maintain contact with the people. That way it wasn't a them-or-us situation. By integrating the army with the general population there'd be less chance of a military crackdown on the civilians.

At the same time the ZIS chief was in charge of all military operations, preventing the two formerly separate outfits from working against each other.

So far the war had been kept away from the capital, but that could change any day or any night.

That was why yachts and fishing boats in the Zandeville harbor were always kept fueled. Just in case. And that was why the civilians kept loaded shotguns and pistols at their sides.

Just in case.

Patrol boats with quick-reaction teams cruised offshore, now and then dropping off teams for random searches.

Despite the relative calm that settled over Zandeville, it was only a matter of time before Fowler moved against the capital.

THE WHITE-WASHED STONE of the presidential palace was an architectural blend of the White House and Heinrich Fowler's personal version of Valhalla. Massive columns flanked a long promenade that led to the main entrance. Domed roofs and elaborately buttressed palace wings gave the complex the aura of power, the home of the Zandesian elite whose windowed offices and suites looked down at the streets of Zandeville.

But it was an illusory power.

Many of the offices were empty. With Emil Nashonge in hiding, many of his hangers-on had been swept out of the palace. Fowler's entire infrastructure of private guards and assistants had also been banished, although many of them had taken their leave the night of the inaugural massacre. Now they were underground in Zandeville or actively supporting Fowler at one of his desert strongholds.

Flags and banners hung from the roofs; sculptured eagles sat perched atop the sprawling palace grounds; the busts of warriors, knights and tribal chieftains gazed down upon the palace courtyard.

All the pomp and circumstance befitted the chivalrous *reich* of Heinrich Fowler and Emil Nashonge. It still would have been regal except for the most recent additions made by the security forces.

Fence shields had been erected on the balconies to deflect grenades; armed ZIS guards steadily patrolled the walkways around the palace grounds; sandbags lined the guardhouse by the main gates, which were always kept closed now.

The road leading up to the gates was blocked with concrete guiders that prevented vehicles from launching a direct assault.

Inside the presidential palace the mood was equally somber. Many of the current residents were Zandesian diplomats, businessmen and FEP activists who were considered particular targets of Fowler's Desert Knights.

Floodlights lit up the courtyard and the outer gates, casting an artificial dawn upon the convoy of Land Rovers and troop carriers that wound through the obstacles at three in the morning.

The convoy had met Molembe's troops upon their return to the airport, ferrying the wounded to the hospital before delivering Molembe's most trusted men to the palace.

In the middle of the convoy was a truckload of prisoners under armed guard, who'd be quartered at the palace with the utmost secrecy and interrogated a lot more fully. Though they'd already answered a lot of questions, there was someone at the palace who could decide how truthful they were.

JANELLE VALLOIS LAY in her bed dreaming. Her legs kicked the silk sheets as if she were trying to walk away from the dream, but there was no escape.

Every night it was the same. A car pulled up at the edge of the crowd that surrounded the presidential platform erected for Leopold Sabda's address to the people. It was a long black limo with tinted windows that nudged the edge of the crowd. No one moved for it.

At first.

A huge throng had come to see democracy dawning over Zandesi and nothing could move them.

Nothing but bullets.

The doors to the limo sprouted open like wings. Two men on each side poured from the car and took cover behind the armor-reinforced doors. Then they opened fire. Not at the presidential platform, but at the people.

They mowed down the Zandesians in a relentless harvest that forced many of them toward the platform to escape the lead scythes.

Civilians were pushed against the picket line of security men in a tidal wave of humanity. Men and women spilled up the stairs, and soon the entire platform was overrun, ready to collapse.

Sabda's presidential bodyguard had suddenly become a uniformed island at the center of chaos, and everyone headed for them. The human flood pressed in on them as they screamed for help, effectively immobilizing them.

Then flashes of fire appeared from several spots in the crowd as gunmen revealed their weapons and almost casually began firing. Fowler's assassins were sprinkled all throughout the audience. En masse they aimed at the UN observers who'd stood at the front of the platform. They went down in waves, observing the fanatic lengths Heinrich Fowler would take to keep his candidate in power.

Janelle was in the middle of the platform, two rows behind Sabda. She was there in her official capacity as liaison between the newly formed government of Zandesi and the U.S. embassy.

But as Sabda's protégée, she was much more than liaison. In her unofficial capacity she served as protocol officer, public-relations specialist and campaign manager. Descended from French landowners, she was a full-fledged Zandesian. One who saw a chance to bring democracy to the country.

In Leopold Sabda she had seen a man who could lead Zandesi to freedom.

But then he became a captive right in front of her eyes.

Sabda and his closest advisers moved toward one side of the stage, gesturing at the helicopter that was circling overhead.

The helicopter descended, hovering at the edge of the platform. Sabda's advisers started climbing into the open cabin. The chopper crew helped them scramble aboard, lifting off as soon as Sabda was inside.

And then she heard shouting from inside the chopper. Fowler's men had managed to climb aboard. They knew of the escape plans, and had worked their way through the crowd to board the helicopter with the president....

There were gunshots, screams, then three bodies were tossed out of the helicopter as it awkwardly rose in the air.

The chopper flew like a heavy metal leaf, listing to the left and right as it sank gradually toward the ground. But then it leveled out and managed to fly over the courtyard gates, finally touching down in the street where several of Fowler's vehicles awaited them.

They took Sabda away.

And they also took Janelle's peace of mind. Because in her dreams one of Fowler's gunmen pointed the barrel of a machine gun in her face... and fired.

She screamed, and the shots stopped as she snapped awake, sitting straight up in bed.

Then she discerned the heavy rappings on the door. Someone was knocking, softly calling her name.

"It's all right, Janelle! It's only me."

She recognized the voice, but she was still caught up in the dream fugue. The killer had seemed so real that his dream shadow was still affecting her, weighing her down.

"Open the door. Please. It's me, Martin."

She drifted out of the bed like a woman who'd just come back from the grave. She shrugged into a light silk robe, opened the door, then stood in the shadow of the Zandesian giant.

"What's wrong?"

She shook her head, unable to speak.

His arms reached out to her, and she fell into them like a child. Nothing romantic could ever pass between them. Martín Molembe had been her mentor, cultivating her, leading her into Leopold Sabda's circle. She saw him as a brother, a brother who'd returned from war.

His face was tired, caked with grime, sweat and innumerable cuts and burns from the field. She realized he'd just come back from fighting the mercenaries in the desert, while all she'd been fighting were the phantoms haunting her dreams.

"I was..." She faltered. It sounded so weak. "I was dreaming. That's why I was screaming. I was dreaming about the day they took Leopold."

"We all have those dreams," he said. "They'll stop soon. And that's a promise. I know it's late, but right now I want you to come downstairs and see a man who's going to help me see that promise through."

"What's his name?" she said.

"That's a good question. At the moment we're calling him Michael Belasko. He's an American on loan."

"The Americans promised us troops, hardware, soldiers."

"That they did," Molembe agreed. "And in a way, that's what they sent us. I've seen him in the field, and I'll tell you one thing. I'm glad he's on our side. He's a hard man to kill."

"But you could kill him?"

"If I had to," he replied. "I'd try. It would be a close call."

She nodded and swept her hair back over her shoulder. The longer she was awake, the stronger she began to feel. She was anchored in the real world once again.

"He wants to see you, Janelle."

"I want to see no one. Tell him I'll see him in the morning. When I'm good and ready."

Molembe shrugged. "He's most persuasive. And he doesn't do things without a good reason. It will be worth it to all of us."

THE EXECUTIONER STOOD at the bottom of the winding stairs and looked up at the thirtyish black-haired woman escorted by Martin Molembe.

Her shoulder-length hair framed a narrow face with almond eyes awash with worry and lack of sleep.

Despite the obvious exhaustion, she still had an elfin beauty about her, enhanced by the slender but statuesque figure beneath her robe.

A petite Parisienne, he thought. Here in the presidential palace she looked more like a debutante than one of the Desert Knights' "Most Wanted" women.

The scowl the woman had prepared for her uninvited guest melted away when she saw him.

Bolan hadn't changed his gear yet. He still wore his desert garb, caked with the debris of war. Maybe that had something to do with her change of demeanor, the warrior thought. She could see they were each fighting the war in their own way.

"And you are?" she said when she reached the bottom of the stairs.

"I'm here to see you. The name is Michael Belasko."

The corners of her mouth turned up in a slight smile. "Of course. Martin has told me about you." Her eyes sparked with interest as she appraised the Executioner. "What could you possibly want with me at this hour?"

"The possibilities are endless," Bolan said, locking onto her gaze. "But for now let's just say that I want your cooperation. There are some prisoners I'd like you to see—"

As though a dark curtain had dropped, the glow in her eyes quickly faded.

"I'd rather not."

"It's more a matter of need than desire," Bolan said. "The prisoners we brought back are mercenaries in the employ of Heinrich Fowler. Naturally all of them say they had nothing to do with the massacre.

Just as naturally we want people who witnessed the massacre to view them to see if they're telling the truth."

"And if they are?"

Bolan paused. "It's a calculated gamble. Martin and I have worked something out that could be to all of our advantage."

"Monsieur Belasko has some ideas I think are worth listening to," the Zandesian Intelligence chief said. "In here." He led the way to a pair of double doors.

A guard stepped aside as they entered a sparsely furnished room that had been an office for one of Emil Nashonge's underlings.

Photographs, plaques, figurines and an elaborately scrolled, gold-lettered nameplate of the former occupant were piled unceremoniously in a box in the corner of the room. Now it was Spartan and functional, reflecting the down-to-earth nature of its current occupant.

Bolan and Janelle dropped into the two pastel-colored chairs that faced the desk.

Molembe headed toward a small serving cart at the side of the room with a tea setting and hot plate. He flicked on the hot plate, started brewing a pot of tea, then sat behind his desk. He clasped his hands on the desk top and leaned forward, covering his reflection on the glossy surface.

"Well," he said, "now we can begin our summit meeting."

"One long overdue," Janelle replied. "It's rare to see you at your desk these days. Too rare."

Molembe gave her a sharp look, which the woman ignored.

"There's too much at risk when you're in the field," she said.

"It's where I belong."

"Under normal circumstances, yes. But the fact is, Martin, that aside from a few paper shufflers, right now I'm looking at the entire government of Zandesi. We must consider the possibility that Leopold may never come back. And if you are killed, what then?"

Bolan saw why Janelle had risen so far. She wasn't just a pretty face or figurehead. Sabda had groomed her to be a devil's advocate. She had the intellect and the courage to challenge anyone.

Molembe tried to evade her question. "We came here to discuss another matter." He nodded at Bolan. "Let's talk about the prisoners."

"She's right," Bolan said. "We know Fowler's strategy is to draw your troops into the desert and keep them tied up in a guerrilla war. If he manages to kill you in the bargain, what's to keep him from killing Sabda and his cabinet? In the chaos that follows, the people might welcome Fowler and Nashonge."

"If it's necessary to go back to the field," Molembe said, "then I'll go. There are risks no matter where we fight from. And yes, Monsieur Belasko, I realize I'm a target. But I should be quite safe with you protecting my back."

"I usually work on the front lines," Bolan said. "I'm a soldier, not a bodyguard."

"Understood. Now, back to the reason why we're here—"

"Yes," Janelle said. "You woke me up to make me a special brew of tea."

Molembe laughed. He went over to the stand and poured tea into small round cups, which he handed to Janelle and Bolan before returning to his desk with his own.

"Now," he said, raising his teacup, "we can begin." He nodded toward Bolan.

The Executioner outlined the plan he and Molembe had developed. In exchange for full disclosure of their mercenary operations, the prisoners would be released.

Using her contacts and, if necessary, those of the U.S. covert community, a well-publicized press conference would be broadcast around the world. Such a move would demonstrate the legitimacy of the government of Zandesi and their willingness to end the war.

"And if it backfires?" Janelle asked. "This could attract the kind of people we don't want. Some mercenaries could see this as a recruiting drive. Or if they are strong enough, maybe even view Zandesi as ripe for their own coup."

"The best way to fight mercenaries is to hit them before they get here," Bolan told her. "Spare these prisoners, and it might save us from fighting a hundred more recruits from the outside world. Mercenaries aren't all killers for hire. If some of them see what's happening, they might stay away. And the ones who ignore the message, well, they'd come no matter what we did."

"I still don't like the risk."

"Don't forget our other targets," Bolan said. "Even if this doesn't stem the flow of mercs, it will still help us with rebel forces. All those who give up their arms will be granted amnesty. At the same time it shows the world that the caretaker government is genuine in its quest for peace. It gives us the higher moral ground."

"And from there," Molembe added, "we can take better aim at our real enemies—those who continue the fight. While I, too, share some of your doubts,

Janelle, politically, in the eyes of the international community, this is the best weapon we have."

"*Politically,* Martin, you aren't that experienced. I still think this sets a dangerous precedent. The mercenary element will come to expect this from us. They'll think they can exploit this weakness the next time."

"They'll be dealt with harshly next time," Molembe argued. "That's something we'll make clear in the press conference. But mercy is called for in this case. Most of these mercenaries were green and had little idea of what was expected from them. For all they knew they were here to support President Sabda."

"Or assassinate him," she said.

"That's why we want you to take a look at them before we go ahead."

"Okay." She tilted her cup and drained the last of her tea as if it was a shot of liquid courage. "Let's get it over with."

A LINE OF MERCENARIES stood side by side in the narrow single cells flanking both sides of the wide corridor in the basement of the presidential palace.

At the moment it had a courthouse atmosphere, with all of the hardmen waiting for the verdict to come down. Their whispered voices and mutters traveled from cell to cell as they watched the small party that had entered the holding room, looking for clues to their fate.

Some of them looked at the SMGs carried by the two uniformed guards. Others were drawn to the black-haired woman whose eyes kept sweeping the room. To men in their straits she was as beautiful as a dream, but a dream dreamt by others. But eventually most of the men turned their attention to Martin Molembe. The huge Zandesian had shown no indication of his plans for the prisoners, and his eyes gave away nothing as he scanned the cells.

Nor was there any comfort to be found from the tall American who stood next to the Zandesian. His stone-cold sniper's eyes seared right through them.

"Listen carefully to me," Molembe bellowed. "Listen as if I were pronouncing the words of the last rite."

It had the desired effect. The mercenaries fell silent, wondering just how close they were to the final ceremony threatened by the ZIS chief.

"There are two ways out of here," the man continued. He gestured to the windowless metal door at the far end of the corridor. "That way lies the graveyard. These men will be your escorts."

Both guards stepped forward, crisply raising their submachine guns until the barrels pointed waist high at the prisoners.

Though they were mostly new to the mercenary game, every man knew the fate of many a gun for hire. An informal firing squad would terminate their stay.

The threat of certain death put them in a cooperative mood. Not a man moved.

"There's another door you can take. You can walk right through the same door we came in through, then you can keep going. We'll get you to the airport and fly you right out of here."

A bitter laugh came from the cell nearest the door. It was the Australian mercenary, looking right at home as he gripped the metal bars. So far the only thing he'd told them was his name. Nicholas Croy.

With a tobacco-baked voice that sounded as if he were in charge, totally unfazed by his situation, Croy said, "What do we have to give up?"

"The truth."

"The truth, eh?" Croy stepped back from the bars. His stubby trigger finger rode the brim of his hat. "Truth's a pretty flexible item."

"Just don't bend it too far," Bolan warned, stepping nearer to the cell.

"Who's this?" Croy asked. "I thought you gave the orders."

"I do." Molembe tipped his head toward Bolan. "And he carries them out. He's the one who'll ask all the questions. He's the one who decides what door you take."

Croy shrugged, acting as if the presence of the Executioner made no difference to him, although he'd obviously been sizing Bolan up ever since he'd walked in.

But the presence of Janelle Vallois did have an effect on the Australian free-lancer. When he noticed how she was carefully checking out the prisoners at the other end of the corridor, a wary look came over his eyes. He tilted his brim down and stared straight ahead.

Janelle moved slowly around the room, finishing her study of the prisoners. None of them provoked a reaction from her. Until she came to Croy.

Her face blanched, and she stepped back instinctively, putting the guards between herself and the cell.

"What is it?" Bolan asked.

She pointed a finger at the Australian. At first she didn't say a word, but her eyes made the accusation just the same.

"Recognize him?"

She nodded. "He was there, at the inauguration. He was shooting at everyone—"

"That's a lie!" Croy snapped. He white-knuckled the bars and pulled himself forward, spitting out his hatred. "You believe a damned woman? Let a woman do your dirty work for you—"

"Shut it," Bolan growled. He unholstered the Beretta 93-R and tapped the barrel against the iron bars.

Croy backed away.

"Take a good, hard look," Bolan advised the woman. "Are you sure he's the one?"

"Yes!" she hissed. "Of course I'm sure! He tried to kill me from the helicopter."

"You're out of your bloody mind," Croy muttered, shaking his head. "If I was gunning for you, honey, you'd be worm bait now...." He looked pointedly toward Bolan, then said, "Attracting a different sort of maggot entirely."

"You can quit the act anytime," Bolan said. "We get the idea you're a tough bastard."

"It's no act. I come from a long line of sons of bitches."

"Maybe," Bolan said. "Fact is, you gave up when you had a chance to die in battle."

"We Croys are crazed, not crazy. I wasn't in a dying mood."

"Killing's more your style," Bolan said. "Especially women."

"The lady's mistaken. And it's damned obvious why. Every man with a gun looks alike when you're on the receiving end. It wasn't me. I came in with this lot."

Bolan targeted the man in the next cell, a thin, sunburned man who looked as though he wished he could go back in time and abort the mission in Zandesi. "Is that true?" Bolan asked.

The man was eager to please. Without missing a beat, he said, "It could be. The first time I saw Croy was in the desert. We all met at the same time out in the Harana."

Bolan checked the story with the other prisoners. All of them remembered seeing Croy come in with a few other mercs, who were also new to the region.

Fresh blood for Fowler's machine.

"Look," Croy said, "I admit I was with Fowler before that. I'm no saint, but I don't go in for slaughter. The helicopter attack, the murder of the UN observers, all that was done by a special unit. Me, I'm just a desert rat."

"Tell me about it," Bolan prompted.

"I said all I got to say."

"For now."

The Executioner conferred with Molembe and Janelle in a low voice. The Zandesian officer repeated his offer. Leniency in exchange for candor. The rest of the hardmen all jumped at the chance.

But Croy remained silent.

A few moments later the guards began escorting the mercenaries outside, taking them down to the debriefing rooms where ZIS men waited for them.

Within five minutes only Bolan and the Australian mercenary were left in the holding room. The Executioner held the key to his cell, spinning the large key ring on his finger, producing a hypnotic effect on the prisoner.

"Is this your idea of torture?" Croy asked. "It's pretty lame, mate."

"I don't kill unless I have to. The way it goes down is up to you."

Croy stepped back from the bars. "If you want to kill me, kill me." He lifted his arms over his head and spun around so his back was to Bolan. "If this makes it easier for you, be my guest."

The Executioner's mirthless laugh echoed in the room. He holstered his Beretta and said, "Turn around, Croy. We both know the game we have to play here. You act like you're ready to go to the grave with your secrets, and I act like I just might be ready to bargain. Sooner or later we strike a deal. Isn't that right?"

Croy returned to his former position near the bars. "That depends on the deal."

"It's simple enough," Bolan said. "You talk, you walk—after the smoke clears. *And* if your story checks out. Right now I'm prepared to believe you weren't involved in the massacre in the square."

"Why's that?"

"If you were sent to hit Janelle, and you missed at that range, I don't think Fowler would have brought you aboard."

"Thanks for the vote of confidence."

"Don't thank me just yet," Bolan went on. "If it turns out you've been lying to me, if we find out in any way that you misled us, well, the ZIS has a fatal cure for that."

"Trust me, mate," Croy said. Like a neighbor chatting over a fence, the man's arms slid through the bars. He idly clasped his hands together for support.

Or for a two-handed sucker punch if Bolan got too close. Despite his air of unconcern, the Executioner knew the man was just waiting for an opening.

"So," Croy said, "let's see if we got anything to talk about. What do you want to know?"

"Let's start with the desert. After your unit was taken prisoner, you didn't seem too surprised to see a second force of Desert Knights."

"That's right, mate. I take life as it comes."

"How about death?"

"That, too, if it has to be."

"Anything can be arranged."

Croy shrugged. "Yeah, well, that's a problem for me right now," he said, looking at the Beretta. "I don't like dealing with a man with a gun. Kind of takes away the spirit of the thing."

"Everything's open to negotiation. If this makes it easier for you to talk, then I'm all for it." Bolan slid off the shoulder rig, carried the weapon to the far side of the room and leaned it against the metal door. Then he returned to the cell. "You were saying?"

"I was saying I got nothing to say. Yet." The Aussie studied Bolan carefully, his eyes gauging the man. The Executioner had made one concession. How far could he push it?

"It's time you laid your cards on the table, Nick. I got places to go—"

"Places to go, people to kill," Croy taunted.

"Don't have to go too far for that. It's time, Nick. You talk or I walk—and then you swing."

"All right," Croy said. "Here's the deal. Like I said, Fowler has special units for special tasks. He's got teams in the city. He's got troops in the field. He's got plans you never dreamed of. But if you want to know what they are, you open the door, give me a shot at my assignment."

"Which is?"

"To kill you," Croy said.

"Are you telling me this has all been a ruse to get you inside the palace? That Fowler sacrificed all those men for that?"

"There's a lot I could tell you, but you've got to open the door to find out."

The Executioner studied the Aussie predator. Croy was about two hundred pounds of brute muscle, a man who had bulled and battled his way across Africa after fleeing his native land one step ahead of the law. He knew the type, knew what they could do.

"You got a deal, Nick." Bolan keyed the lock, and the door swung inward.

Croy wasted no time. Like iron drawn to a magnet, his ham fist whipped toward Bolan's face, the motion seeming to propel him from the cell.

Bolan let it come, twisting to the right at the last instant, letting the blow glance off his cheek.

As Croy's momentum carried him forward, closing for the kill, Bolan kept on spinning to his right. His rigid right elbow swung around like a war hammer, picking up speed and power until it crashed into the underside of Croy's jaw.

The impact lifted the man off his feet. His broad-brimmed hat sailed to the floor as his head tilted back, blood fountaining from his mouth like an oil strike.

Bolan continued his move, unfolding his arm and snapping a fist to Croy's face. His knuckles caught him in the bridge of his nose, producing a sharp crack.

At the end of his split-second maneuver, Bolan stepped forward and closed the gap with the falling man. This wasn't a friendly contest. There were no times-out. The object was to take the man down as fast as possible, then make sure he stayed there.

Bolan went straight for the dazed man's gut with a front snap kick. Nothing fancy, just a plain, curled-toe pickax to the abdomen.

Croy took the hit dead-on and bounced back against the wall. He hung there suspended for a moment, like a freeze frame from a road accident. Then he fell like a diver onto the concrete floor, flat on his ruined face.

A stream of blood reddened the floor around his head. The Aussie groaned. He couldn't get up, nor could he retreat into unconsciousness.

Bolan dropped into a half crouch and pressed his right knee into Croy's back. "Game's over, Nick. Next move's final. You decide."

Croy grunted his assent.

The Executioner backed away and gave him room to move. Not that moving was all that easy for Croy.

Bolan had executed the techniques in little more than a second. Like a surgical strike, it had taken the fight out of the man and perhaps saved them hours of "negotiating."

Croy stirred slowly. He stretched his arms and legs. Then, like a man coming back from the dead, he crawled to the rear of the cell. He grabbed the edge of the cot and managed to pull himself into a sitting position.

"I kept my part of the bargain," Bolan said. "Now you keep yours. Start talking."

Croy tilted his head back, then ran his cuff across his face to wipe off some of the blood. He shook his head slowly from side to side. "Damn," he said. "You're just like Fowler. You had this figured out all along."

His words came out slowly. Like a drunkard's, the Aussie's speech was slurred and broken.

But Bolan sat there patiently, taking the time to piece it together. With all the hard Intel Croy was divulging, it sounded just like music to his ears.

6

Sea breezes washed over the immense body of Emil Nashonge as he paced the well-shaded veranda and looked out at the ocean. The diamond-capped waters of the Atlantic beckoned to the deposed head of state.

Hissing surf called to him.

But it was a call he couldn't respond to. All he could do was scowl. The water wasn't for him, nor was the open air that rushed through the leaves of the palms that stood like graceful sentinels posted all around the villa.

During the daylight hours his unmistakable profile wasn't supposed to be seen away from the screened-in veranda on the second floor of the secluded villa. Nor could he walk the terraced grounds.

Such simple pleasures were forbidden him, on the order of Heinrich Fowler, kingmaker, life taker. The man had left complete instructions about every aspect of Nashonge's life.

He had no illusions about the danger he was in. Leopold Sabda wasn't the only leader in captivity. Fowler controlled every move that Nashonge made, every breath he took.

The safe house was a prison.

In ordinary times the villa on the outskirts of Zandeville would be a paradise. Like stepping-stones, the plushly landscaped tiers led down to the sea. From the bottom tier a wooden stairway descended to the private beach and dock where a cabin cruiser and speedboat glinted in the sunlight.

Despite the sleek fishing poles that adorned the cockpits like radar, they weren't strictly luxury boats. Below decks and concealed in the paneling were weapons caches, communications gear and the most important survival tool of all—U.S. dollars, gold coins. Wherever flight took them, they'd survive.

These weren't ordinary times. This was war, and the government of Emil Nashonge had been one of the first casualties. Here in exile he was a powerless observer.

On paper the villa belonged to a French businessman who'd been co-opted by Heinrich Fowler years ago. But the Frenchman rarely showed his face at the deceptively calm concentration camp.

It was staffed entirely by Fowler's mercenaries, who watched his every move—not a difficult task when their prisoner was a man of his girth. Nashonge had allowed himself to become obese. And not just his body. For years his thinking had also grown flabby. Anytime he had problems he turned them over to Fowler, who eagerly solved them.

Before he realized it, he'd turned over the government to Heinrich Fowler.

And finally he'd given up his freedom.

To the outside world the staff attending to Nashonge's needs appeared to be nothing more than servants. But they were also professional killers.

Every time he heard their footsteps he wondered if that was the last sound he'd hear. Were they waiting on him, bringing him the meat, fruit and alcohol that made up his customary diet? Or were they drawing their weapons as they approached, bringing him the ultimate peace?

Fowler had prepared several different scenarios for his return to power. Nashonge would either be the hero or the fall guy, whatever it took for Fowler to accomplish his goals. There was no guarantee that Nashonge would ever return from exile. He could very easily become one of the disappeared ones, the troublemakers who just vanished from the earth and were never heard of again.

Nashonge had rubber-stamped the practice years earlier. Since then, Fowler had used it to purge the government of Nashonge's enemies, and his friends. He was adrift in a government run by another man.

With a gargantuan sigh Nashonge left the veranda and walked back into the air-conditioned interior. It was time to watch the news and find out what was happening in the country.

As he passed the television set he grabbed the remote control, flicked it like a magic wand, then dropped into the extrawide chair to watch the newscast.

A familiar apparition appeared on the screen.

It was the face of Martin Molembe. On-screen was a blowup of a photograph of Molembe that had appeared throughout the world press. His name was now on the lips of every Zandesian. Soon it would be known worldwide. The man was grooming himself to fill the vacuum. While he proclaimed to the world his efforts in saving President Sabda, he was in reality paving the way for his own presidency.

It wouldn't be so bad, Nashonge thought, to be followed in office by Martin Molembe. The country would thrive... Odd, he thought. He so rarely thought about the people, about the place of Zandesi in the world. But now that it was taken from him, he couldn't help thinking of all the things he could have done, the mark he could have made. Instead of opting for a presidential paradise, he could have opened the gates to his own people. Shared the wealth... He shook his head. Such dreams were for men like Leopold Sabda and Martin Molembe, whose face seemed to grow godlike as the camera moved in for a close-up.

"Hail Caesar," Nashonge muttered.

The photo showed Molembe with a gentle expression and a hint of a tired smile on his face, like a postcard from a long-lost friend. In a way that's just what it was.

In the old days Martin Molembe had been a friend. Several times he'd counseled Nashonge against giving Heinrich Fowler such free rein, and Molembe had always been adamant about the people deserving honest rule. He'd pressured Nashonge to take control back from Fowler, to give the people a voice.

But Nashonge had taken the easy way. He'd gone along with Fowler's plans, and now his friendship with Molembe was gone. The leader of the ZIS was with the enemy.

Judging from other news clips he'd seen recently, the ZIS chief wasn't alone in his actions. Most of the Zandesians were his enemy, although to the reporters they always spoke guardedly. After all, there was always a chance that Nashonge could return.

At the moment the chances of a triumphant return seemed slim, Nashonge thought. Not while he was confined to quarters, watched over by men loyal to a usurper.

The screen suddenly changed, showing a brief travelogue of downtown Zandeville, people going about their business, unworried. As the reporter's voice praised Martin Molembe as one of the key figures responsible for maintaining the state of calm so soon after the massacre, the camera panned the presidential palace.

The television camera zoomed through the main entrance and, once inside the palace, took the viewer into the office of Martin Molembe.

Nashonge recognized it instantly, even with all of the plaques, medals and certificates missing from the walls. It was the office of his former chief of staff, a man who was now also in hiding. Or perhaps dead. Nashonge had no way of knowing.

But now the office looked very functional. There was no trace of the ornate trappings so typical when Nashonge had been in residence.

Sitting behind a desk with a sparse top, the head of the ZIS wore an elegantly tailored suit that tempered his military image. Tonight there was a glimpse of the statesman about him.

He spoke in low but confident tones. It was the voice of truth, the voice of a man who had nothing to hide.

A good act, Nashonge thought as he watched Molembe's media performance.

A ZNT logo emblazoned the head of the microphone wielded by the reporter from Zandesi National Television, a thin, earnest-looking man.

"As the highest-ranking member of ZIS, Mr. Molembe, you are currently in charge of keeping the peace *and* conducting the war at the same time." He spoke in the accentless English favored by aspiring international correspondents. "These tasks seem to be at odds with each other."

"Actually they complement each other quite well," Molembe replied. "Here in the city there's a sense of stability. Life goes on. And it goes on very well. That's only possible because of our efforts in the war against the terrorists in the desert."

"That brings us to the unusual decision you made recently when you released several mercenaries taken prisoner during the desert campaign. It seems a strange way of fighting a war, to go out to the desert to capture terrorists only to bring them back to the city and release them. How do you explain that?"

"I'll explain it the same way I did when we released them. It's a way for the legitimate government of Zandesi to get its message out to the people that we don't want war with foreign mercenaries. Nor with our own people who fight alongside them."

"But they went away unpunished," the reporter protested.

"That isn't the way we see it. The mercenaries who were released were misguided. They didn't take part in the inaugural massacre. They didn't even know the reason why they were brought here—until they were forced out into the desert and told to fight. A tragic circumstance for both sides. In this case we'll be merciful. But from here on, let it be known that all mercenaries have been given fair warning. There will be no more releases."

"There has been talk of amnesty."

"So far it's only talk," Molembe replied. "No one has taken us up on our offer. Anyone who wishes to quit the fighting and leave the country is guaranteed safe passage."

"And those who stay?"

"They'll be dealt with according to the rules of war. The government of Zandesi will prevail against those who try to tear it down. The will of the people shall prevail. We will fight to maintain our freedom."

The camera turned toward the reporter, who smiled cynically.

"That sounds all very noble, but how do you address the fears of the people who say that the country is now in the hands of the military—no matter what you choose to call them these days? And they will likely remain in control even if Leopold Sabda is returned."

The question took Molembe by surprise. "That is unthinkable," he said. "It will take me only one second to turn over this job. I'm a soldier, not a politician. The problems facing Zandesi are best solved by the man elected by the people."

"And what if President Sabda doesn't come back to us? He's in dangerous hands."

"Elections will be held," Molembe said. "That is my promise."

"Will your name be on the ballot?"

"I have no interest in running. Only serving."

Emil Nashonge almost found himself believing it. So earnest. So honest. But he knew that no man could refuse power once it was thrust into his hands. He'd do anything to hold on to it.

No matter how genuine Molembe seemed as he voiced his desire to serve the country, there was an echo that only Nashonge could hear.

It was the echo of his own words, uttered so long ago when he'd said similar things to the public.

But Nashonge had succumbed.

And chances were good that Martin Molembe would also fall to the temptations offered him. He, too, would take the necessary steps to hold on to his power no matter how pretty a picture he painted at the moment.

7

The army of looters struck at seven in the evening, when the streets of Zandeville were quiet, the people immersed in the siestalike lull between the end of business hours and the beginning of nightlife.

A battered red pickup truck clattered down the main street, Avenue de Paris, which was the capital's glittering shopping district.

Four men stood in the bed of the truck as it traveled the middle of the street, two men on each side dressed in jeans and T-shirts, looking decidedly out of place in the cosmopolitan center of Zandeville. They looked like refugees from another world, a poisoned universe of murder and terror.

They were smiling, as if they planned on having a good time.

The truck rolled to a stop. Leaning over the side panels of the vehicle for balance and leverage, the men started the festivities by tossing rocks and bricks at the shiny glass windows that offered capitalist glimpses of Paradise.

Bursting glass crashed onto the street from shops lining both sides of the avenue.

The truck began rolling again as the men shouted their war cries.

"Down with Molembe!"

"Smash the regime!"

"Free Zandesi..."

"Free food!" Twisted laughter shrieked from the truck as the men picked up more missiles from the pile of bricks and rocks stacked in the rusty truck bed.

Glass panes shattered in hideous progression, one after the other, crashing and tinkling in harmony.

Two more pickups raced down the street, the men in those vehicles also dressed in plain clothes. But they worked in an organized fashion. Jumping off the trucks, they headed straight for the stores with the ruined facades and grabbed at everything in their path.

It was a choreographed assault.

First the expensive shops were hit. Luxury items were yanked from stores and carried out into the street. Clothes, jewelry, watches, stereos. Those shops that had iron grates protecting them were hit by teams of crowbar-wielding thugs who worked quickly at the bolts, ripping them out of their concrete moorings.

Then the iron frames were pulled free and tossed to the ground with a loud clatter.

Joining the first band of looters were throngs of people who poured out of the modest homes and small informal restaurants on the side streets that led off the shopping district.

At first they came to see what the noise and shouting was about.

But then the looting fever spread, and they stayed to see what they could get for themselves.

With price soaring because of the hoarding instincts of those who could afford to buy the goods, many of the average citizens of Zandeville were doing without. They had less food, less drink, less hope.

But they could make up for their suffering. Another time they might have resisted, but the mob mentality had set in and everyone helped themselves.

Uniformed policemen two blocks over climbed into their car and raced to the first block of Avenue de Paris that was under siege. But the pickup trucks had been abandoned at the end of the street and blocked their way. They had to get out on foot.

A sea of looters swarmed all around them.

Their hands clawed for their side arms, but neither man was willing to shoot. Both were afraid of the violence that might be unleashed.

The sounds of looting from the next block drifted toward the policemen. Another team of cars and pickups had struck a parallel block, turning that into a madhouse.

Sirens sounded in all parts of the city.

Riots had come to the capital, courtesy of Heinrich Fowler's plainclothes anarchists.

"GET READY," Pierre Lauchierre said as he peered out of the mouth of the alley, pushing aside a long lock of black hair that hung down his forehead like a dagger. "Here come the reinforcements."

The first pair of officers on the scene were a half block past them, already swallowed up by the crowd. Their shouts were drowned out by laughter of the crowd, and their threats went unheeded in the passion of looting.

The second pair of officers approached just as tentatively as the first, having left the safety of their patrol car.

Lauchierre exhaled and forced himself to relax. It was always like this before a performance. Before he used his instrument. "Half a minute and they'll be on us."

He wore jeans and a long striped shirt that hung down to the middle of his thighs. The shirt was unbuttoned, revealing a tattered white T-shirt. Though he was dressed like a vagrant, there was a hardness in his eyes seldom seen on the street. The rolled-up shirtsleeves showed a kind of muscle tone few men achieved. Professional tone.

Hidden by his loose shirt was a 9 mm Heckler & Koch automatic pistol just in case he had to use it. The weapon was tucked into a makeshift holster on his belt. It was the same make as the weapons used by the ZIS security force.

The second man was a native Zandesian of much shorter stature. He looked slim, but there was a deceptive strength about him. His name was Jacob and, like Lauchierre, he was a gun for hire. They had both served with Heinrich Fowler in a half-dozen bitter wars. For them, this was just a night on the town.

Jacob was also dressed in plain clothes. His scruffy jeans and ripped T-shirt made him look harmless, like a drunk cut adrift from the mob.

"Now," Lauchierre said. "Now."

"Got ya."

Jacob staggered out into the street with a bottle of beer tilted in his hand. He piloted himself in a drunkard's walk that placed him right in the path of the uniformed ZIS officers. They were moving slower and slower up the street as they approached the riot zone.

"Stand where you are!" the first officer shouted. At first sight of Jacob, his hand instinctively went for his side arm. But when he perceived Jacob's ragged condition he relaxed. He left the weapon holstered, laughed curtly and stiff-armed the vagrant out of the way.

Jacob let himself bounce off the wall. He muttered at the second officer and staggered toward him in his drunkard's walk.

The second officer, a shorter man in a meticulously pressed uniform, made a wide detour around Jacob as if he were a piece of human debris kicking down the street. He dismissed him with a glance and, like his partner, concentrated on the crowd of looters up the block.

The drunk suddenly became dead sober.

Jacob turned the brown bottle upside down and gripped it by the long neck. He took one long step toward the shorter officer and smashed the bottle into the back of the man's head. It made a sickening sound and dropped him like stone.

The impact of the blow made the bottle fly out of Jacob's hand and crash onto the sidewalk where it formed a frothy stain around the head of the fallen officer.

The first officer turned back, and this time his hand was really going for his weapon. But it never made it. Before he could reach his holster there was a blur of motion off to his right.

Lauchierre's right hand knifed out of the alley.

The rigid edge of his palm skimmed across the side of the man's temple, jolting his head back and dislodging his cap. Continuing the move, the mercenary curled his hand around the back of the stunned officer's neck and flung him headfirst into the alley. At the end of the maneuver he twisted his hand slightly and guided the tumbling officer face-first into the brick wall.

He groaned and dropped to the ground.

They dragged the officers into the alley, quickly removed their uniforms and changed them for their own clothes.

A few moments later the two "police officers" came out of the alley and headed for the riot.

Without saying a word they waded into the milling crowd.

Then they began shooting, the 9 mm automatics spitting flame.

It took a while before the people realized what was happening. At first they thought it was just noise and went on with their looting.

But then the constant roar of gunfire and the attendant screams of pain filtered through the chaos.

Like a panicked herd of cattle, the looters ran in all directions, away from the center of danger, away from the uniformed officers who coolly stood there firing at anything that moved.

When it was over there were ten men and women lying dead in the road, trails of blood showing the doomed paths they'd taken as they'd tried to crawl away.

The two real ZIS officers were stunned.

"Why'd you do it?" one of them shouted, his face red with fury. "Why the hell did you fire?"

"Just following orders," Lauchierre replied. "Which reminds me..." He turned the gun on the ZIS officers and squeezed off two quick shots.

The officers dropped to the ground, joining their Zandesian comrades.

The street was empty now, littered with broken bottles and smashed crates, coats, hats and stereos, one of them playing tinny music from an untuned station.

The plunder remained on Avenue de Paris. And all that the survivors really carried with them was the memory of a government gone mad, a government that had begun killing its own people.

THAT NIGHT copies of another communiqué were delivered to embassies in Zandeville and to the television and radio stations.

Soon the audiotape was broadcast around the country, and then it was picked up by the international news services.

It was a joint message from Heinrich Fowler and Leopold Sabda, calling for peace and condemning the brutal actions of the government.

"The slaughter has to stop," Fowler said. "We are willing to do anything we can to bring about peace and restore stable government to Zandesi. The military regime that shed the blood of its own people in the streets of Zandeville must be abolished. Speak your minds and call for the return of peace, the return of Leopold Sabda."

The communiqué ended with Leopold Sabda's voice seconding Fowler's plea. He sounded solemn and sincere as he said, "Raise your voice for freedom. Raise your voice for Leopold Sabda... and Heinrich Fowler."

WITHIN AN HOUR, the official voice of the government of Zandesi responded to the communiqué. Janelle Vallois appeared on-screen in a ZNT broadcast that was fed around the world.

And though it obviously troubled her to do so, she spoke against Leopold Sabda, the man who had groomed her for the role she now had to play.

"The slaughter in the streets tonight was orchestrated by Heinrich Fowler. Every indication points to a military operation carried out by his guns for hire. The ZIS is investigating and has already gathered testimony from witnesses who saw this terrorist action.

"The nearly naked bodies of two brutally slain ZIS officers were found in an alley, indicating that Fowler's confederates murdered the officers and then disguised themselves in official uniforms. It wasn't the government of Zandesi that caused this outrage. It was the work of Heinrich Fowler—his bloody fingerprints are all over this."

Her voice quavered, but she continued. "As far as the plea from Leopold Sabda—I must tell you that it was the voice of terror that you heard tonight. It was the voice of a man with a gun to his head. And that is the only way Fowler wants to hear you speak. Voices raised in terror. In fear."

The broadcast featured several witnesses who recalled seeing the militarylike operation that sparked the looting. It also featured the names of the dead and showed the mourning families. Instead of covering it up, the media showed the street massacre in all of its hideous color.

It was an effective rebuttal, coming so quickly after Fowler's communiqué. The people wanted answers, and Janelle Vallois gave them everything she knew.

But still there was doubt in the minds of some of the people. They'd been lied to so often in the past, it was hard to recognize the truth when it came.

It was all part of the war that was being fought in the streets and in the media.

And right now the government could only claim a slim victory.

LIGHTS FLASHED from the desert below as the drone of the chopper neared the rendezvous point. Like diamonds formed from a coal-black darkness, the twinkling lights seemed to grow larger, forming a T-shaped landing zone.

Laden with fresh ammo cases, water containers and stocks of food, the Westland Lynx came in at an angle, kicking up a rotor-wash trail of grit and sand as it touched down just to the left of the lights.

Then a blanket of darkness fell over the chopper as the lights blinked off.

Now that the Lynx had landed safely, moonlight was all they needed to finish the operation.

As the well-oiled sliding cabin doors rolled open, a half-dozen mercenaries swarmed to the chopper. They unloaded the cases in a hurry and handed them off to another string of men, who carted them off into the darkness.

When the matériel was off-loaded, the replacement cargo headed for the chopper. The "cargo" was a string of well-armed men who'd been standing in the shadows surrounding the chopper.

Heinrich Fowler was in the lead, flanked by Gauclere, his right-hand man. The men were followed by several well-dressed mercenaries who looked distinctly out of place in their shirts and jackets.

It was a good crew, Fowler thought, dressed for a different kind of war. In the city they could pass as businessmen if they had to. Beneath their jackets they packed holstered automatics. In their athletic bags and attaché cases they carried submachine guns and spare clips.

Everything they needed to conduct the business of war.

While the men stowed their gear the copilot of the Serpentine Force helicopter went back to the cabin. His zip jacket was laden with survival gear, and the flap of his side arm holster was open and ready for business. He looked furtive, as if he expected a lightning bolt to strike him at any time.

"Situation report," Fowler said to him.

"Sir, most of your people are already in position—"

"*Our* people," Fowler corrected.

"Yes, sir. Most of our people are in position now or will be by the time we get there."

"And the opposition?"

"Business as usual. No extra patrols. No sign of any unusual troop movements."

"Good." Fowler studied the nervous airman. "And how about you? Any problems?"

He paused. "We've been questioned several times about our performance in the skirmish and why we didn't discover the second body of men. But we held up fine."

"I see. And how about our brave pilot? Does Julian share your confidence?"

"To be honest—"

"If you want to keep on living, that's the only way to be with me," Fowler warned.

"We're both uneasy. Our movements are watched closely. But then, so is everyone who's been brought into the ZIS. The vetting process goes on all the time. However, to our advantage, Molembe has to spread Serpentine Force very thin, chasing after all of the shadows you've created. We can get away when we must."

"Good." Fowler nodded. "I realize you're taking chances." He gripped the man's shoulder. "But high risks bring big rewards."

The copilot nodded.

"All right," Fowler said. "Let's go pay our respects to the good people of Z'ville.''

The copilot went back up to the cockpit.

A smile slowly spread across Fowler's face as the crew prepared to lift off.

Vengeance was coming.

He'd been stung badly by the media war that was raging in the capital. Fowler's initial communiqués featuring his and Sabda's taped pleas for reconciliation had fallen on deaf ears. But Molembe had done quite well in putting out *his* message that all was well.

The staged riots hadn't disrupted the city as much as he'd anticipated. The people still bought Molembe's pitch that everything was under control and there was no need to negotiate with Fowler.

Somehow Molembe and his witch, Janelle Vallois, had convinced them that the riots were a brief aberration, a lamentable tragedy that couldn't happen again.

His contacts in the city informed him that even though there was a lot of grumbling, the majority of Zandesians supported Molembe. The feeling was that if they couldn't ransom Leopold Sabda, they still had a good man in control.

But at least the riots had one good effect. They'd given Fowler's people in Zandeville a chance to observe how well the ZIS responded to emergencies and where some of the quick-reaction teams were located.

It would all even out in the end, Fowler thought. Soon the mood of the people would change. The first stage hadn't gone well. No problem. That was merely a soft probe, a minor stratagem.

Soon he'd be in the city itself, preparing to launch the second stage. Zandeville would have a taste of the anarchy to come, anarchy that could only be vanquished by men like Heinrich Fowler and the Desert Knights.

Yes, the people would welcome him back with open arms once he demonstrated just how out of control the country could get. Then they'd realize it was better to deal with the devil they knew rather than risk the lethal lottery of terror.

The helicopter lifted off like a flying warhorse, angling past the landing zone. Once it was airborne, it headed back the way it had come.

Soon they'd be in the capital, where Heinrich Fowler belonged.

The shuddering aircraft had a soothing effect on Fowler as they left the desert rendezvous behind. The drumming of the rotors was like a lullaby of war.

In a way, part of him was content with how matters turned out. Perhaps he'd sat in the comfortable seat of power too long. Perhaps it was meant for him to spend his forty days in the desert. Even though he kept himself physically sharp, maybe he'd slipped a little mentally.

There was nothing like a full-scale war to bring back a man's senses. Not that he'd been totally idle. Though the Fowler clan had extensive holdings in Zandesian industries, from time to time he had to supplement his fortune by brokering mercenary operations throughout Africa.

His main sphere of influence was the West African coast. The countries to the north and south of Zandesi were always ripe for hired armies or surgical-strike teams. Sometimes he operated in the open. Other times he or his people went in as arms merchants, selling sophisticated weapons along with "paramilitary consultants" to demonstrate their use in live field tests against the enemy.

He'd also performed services for South Africa, having maintained close ties ever since he'd served a tour with the Recce Commandos. Upon his return to Zandesi, he'd carried out a number of low-key operations for the South Africans that couldn't be officially attached to the government. But credit was given to him by those in the know, and his name was whispered by power brokers who worked behind the scenes.

The whispers were good for business. The mercenary market turned out to be a gold mine for Fowler, a hidden network of lost treasures that could only be found by those who had the right key. Fowler had the contacts and the reputation that made other nations eager to buy into the legend.

It was a legend he had to live up to in his own country now. If Zandesi was lost to him, so was the rest of Africa.

The chopper flew north, cutting a wide swath around the corridors patrolled by other units of Serpentine Force.

Two hours had passed by the time the chopper landed in the middle of a field bordering a deserted stretch of road along the northern coast of Zandesi.

From a nearby farm two black cars and a jeep headed down the long driveway that led to the main coastal road. They swung out onto the road, then slowly rolled past the new arrivals who'd disembarked from the chopper.

After both sides checked each other out, Fowler's crew emerged from the shadows and climbed into the cars and jeep.

The helicopter lifted off and headed toward the area it was supposed to be patrolling.

The terror teams were almost in place. Soon they'd make their play.

With their passengers aboard, the cars drove slowly back down the coastline road, a soft parade of assassins. The convoy turned back up the driveway and rolled up to the dimly lit farmhouse.

When Fowler's car stopped, several shapes filtered from the house and from the outbuildings. A small army had gathered in the dark.

Leading them was Gunther Braun, a German national who'd worked with Fowler on several other operations. His blond hair had turned grayish, and his once-lean frame now carried a lot of extra pounds. Braun was a grand old man in the mercenary trade.

Braun and his crew were expensive talent but worth the cost. They handled a good part of Fowler's citywide operations, including the looting spree that had rocked Zandeville.

Fowler and Braun clasped hands, then headed toward the barn off to the left of the main house. Inside was an old Volkswagen van and a beat-up station wagon, both packed with long cardboard boxes.

"How do they look?" Fowler asked.

"Perfect. Right down to the last gold button."

"Good. Let's see them."

Braun smiled. He was long used to Fowler's ways, knowing that the man never took anyone's word for anything. He always had to see for himself.

"Fresh from the warehouse," Braun promised, opening the van doors. "We brought them out this afternoon." He pulled down several of the cardboard boxes and opened them for Fowler's inspection.

Inside the boxes were stolen government uniforms, the trademark police blues of the ZIS. Gold-lettered ZIS insignia emblazoned the brim of the peaked police hats and the shoulder boards and collar tabs on the shirts. Gold buttons gleamed in the moonlight. The newly issued uniforms came complete with wide belt and holster.

"Any security problems?" Fowler said.

"Not unless Molembe's got some necromancers on his team. Our inside man 'disappeared' shortly after he smuggled the uniforms to us."

"How tragic."

"Actually it was kind of fun. As a reward for his services, we took him out for some deep-sea fishing."

"And?"

"And he made excellent bait."

Fowler nodded his approval. "Excellent." Then he looked out into the darkness where the troops had gathered.

"Well, what are you waiting for? Enlist these men into the ZIS."

Braun called out to his men. In just a few minutes they had transformed themselves into crisply dressed ZIS officers.

Then Fowler and some of the Desert Knights he'd brought with him changed into the official uniforms. He tucked his coil of hair down the back of his collar, tilted his brim hat forward and put on a pair of glasses.

Satisfied he wouldn't be recognized, Fowler conducted a brief inspection of the others. When they passed muster, he turned his attention to a small group of men who'd stayed in their plain clothes.

At their head was Gauclere, still looking as though he was ready for a night on the town.

Fowler pulled Gauclere and the others off to the side. "You know your targets?" he asked.

"I've been dreaming about it," Gauclere replied, "every step of the way." The other men nodded. They, too, had already lived out the mission in their heads. Now all they had to do was play it out on the world stage.

"All right," Fowler said, "get on with it. It's time to make your dreams come true. You'll have a ten-minute head start before we bring in the cavalry."

GAUCLERE BOBBED HIS HEAD to the beat of the music booming from the Ocean Top club at the end of the pier. He'd ordered a drink at the bar, flirted with a barmaid, then turned his attention to the dance floor as if he were just one more man searching for romance.

The elegant club was favored by Zandeville's *grand monde,* the high society who clung to its comfortable world no matter where the war raged.

Just like every other night, the club was packed. It was a place where the upper-class movers and shakers of Zandeville came to be seen.

And, Gauclere thought, it was a place where they could go out in style.

The mercenary sipped his drink slowly, looking around the club at the other men who'd entered with him. They were sitting at a small table alongside the dance floor, glasses of champagne in front of them, waiting for his cue.

THE BLUE-UNIFORMED Desert Knights drifted down the coastline in twos and threes, moving inexorably toward their soft targets. The beachhead brigade, Fowler thought as he watched his men trudging through the sand, stopping and taking up their positions.

Atlantic surf thrashed and hissed on the shore. Steel-drum-and-guitar music drifted from the seaside hotels and nightclubs, some of them on stilts, as if they were gracefully walking out into the water.

From their tables and booths came lilting feminine laughter and the clink of ice-filled glasses, the sounds of nightlife blending with the music.

It was a beautiful sight.

Especially when viewed through a sniper scope.

Heinrich Fowler swept his Belgian FN FAL 7.62 mm rifle from left to right, picking out dance partners for the fatal waltz.

The cross hairs in the illuminated scope drifted over the bare and lovely shoulders of Zandesian women in their gowns and the European émigrés who'd made Zandesi their home long ago.

Before the night was through they'd wish they'd never come here. The people of Zandeville would fear both rebels and government troops alike.

It would be a night to remember.

Fowler hummed along with the music that drifted from the nightclub. It had a catchy beat. Soon the dancers would move faster—once he added some 9 mm counterpoint.

THE WOMAN GLIDED across the dance floor of the Ocean Top, a vision in red.

In her midthirties, Lydia, as she was known, still held on to the beauty that had made her a prize in every capital in Europe. Her face was smooth, her eyes daring, her voluptuous figure wrapped in red satin.

A prize to the well-off men in the Ocean Top circle, a trophy for Gauclere. Like a hypnotized man he watched her move with her partner. His hand was on her hip, and now and then his lips upon her neck.

But she turned this way and that, breaking away from his grasp every few steps.

She was an exquisite and potent symbol of Zandeville royalty, and she was about to be dethroned.

Gauclere finished his drink, wiped his lips with his napkin, then reached inside his jacket to pull out a .45 automatic.

Pivoting to his right, Gauclere fired at the woman. The heavy slug shattered her head like a melon, spraying her dying thoughts over her partner.

The man stared in shock and fear, but only for a moment. The next round caught him in the chest. He flew back, dancing around like a blood-spattered puppet before he fell to the floor.

The stampede had begun.

Gauclere's companions had pushed their table aside, raised their weapons and begun to fire.

One after the other the high-born died.

The band threw down their instruments and ran for cover, their screams joining the rest.

Splashes sounded from outside the club as the patrons jumped into the water. Some of them missed, thunking onto the gleaming power boats moored there.

And inside the club the dance of death went on.

IT WAS TIME. Fowler exhaled softly as he pulled the trigger of his FN FAL rifle.

The woman was sitting alone at her table, her drink halfway to her mouth, when the shots rang out.

She screamed as the glass shattered and fountained her bright green drink into the air. Then the bullet passed on to the next target, a waiter who'd taken his last order. He fell back with red ribbons of blood seeping down his collar.

The woman jumped to her feet and danced around the slain man. She looked toward the beach where the shot had come from, then looked around wildly for help.

Fowler adjusted his aim and squeezed off another round.

The woman shook as if she'd received an electric shock. She took several staggering steps, then fell to the floor dead, a blossoming bullet hole drenching her white cotton with red.

''Thanks for the dance,'' Fowler muttered.

The crack of rifle fire sounded up and down the beach as the Desert Knights opened up at random.

Then they stormed the clubs, hurtling through the brightly lit alcoves, their official uniforms giving the club goers hope that the madness was over.

But then the blue-uniformed men opened fire, as if they were in a panic. They fired at anything that moved. The saviors had turned into slaughterers.

After wreaking havoc at the clubs, the fake ZIS teams went in pursuit of the mercenaries who'd started the panic.

The streets were alive with screams and gunfire. And blue uniforms.

Then it ended as quickly as it had started. The marauders vanished into safehouses, discarding their uniforms and waiting for the inevitable chaos that would follow.

Madness and murder had come to the capital.

8

The hooded rider approached the ZIS picket line and raised his right hand in greeting. He did so slowly, aware of the guns pointed at him from within the desert outpost.

The pickets were also aware of the long line of Maskarai horsemen who fanned out behind the first rider, cradling their rifles in the event things turned ugly.

Word spread quickly inside the camp, and in a few moments Captain Tsawa, commander of Molembe's desert troops, arrived at the gate.

Tsawa recognized the bronzed rider from the day he and his tribesmen had been captured by the ZIS commandos—captured and released on the condition they wouldn't ride against Molembe again.

"Let him pass," Tsawa ordered.

A handful of men in desert-camouflage fatigues opened the barricades and let the horseman enter.

"What do you want?" Captain Tsawa asked, shielding his eyes from the sun as he looked up at the tribesman.

"Molembe," Zhoave responded.

"I see." At the moment Molembe was spearheading a sweep through the city, searching for the gunmen who'd laid waste to Zandeville's gold-coast resorts—uniformed gunmen. Until they devised a way to fight back at the death squads, the city would be in chaos. And all the blame would fall on Molembe. "He's not available."

"I have to talk to him."

"First you have to talk to me," Tsawa said. "This way." He pointed toward a shelter that was little more than brush and netting draped over several six-foot-high posts.

The Maskarai tribesman looked down at Captain Tsawa, then reluctantly dismounted and followed him. He looped the reins of his horse around one of the posts and stepped inside the shade.

"Please," Tsawa said, "make yourself comfortable." He gestured at one of the benches that had been formed from empty ammo boxes.

"Most luxurious quarters." Zhoave smiled as he sat across from Captain Tsawa.

"Now, why have you come?"

The tall Maskarai warrior studied Tsawa, taking his measure before committing himself. "My people have been approached by Fowler's colonials again. They wish to strengthen their forces with our riders. They need us to protect their hostages while they go to fight on the coast."

Tsawa nodded. The Maskarai had a centuries-long history as superb horse soldiers. They fought on horseback and they often negotiated on horseback, which showed how sincere Zhoave was in wanting to strike a deal. He'd dismounted to accept the Spartan hospitality of the ZIS captain.

"What have you told Fowler's men?"

"That we will join them," Zhoave said. "And that is why I must talk with Molembe. We want only to join Fowler's people to destroy them. Word has reached us that the German's troops were responsible for the massacre of our people—and not the ZIS."

"We already told you that."

"Yes," Zhoave replied. "And now we were told by our own people, Maskarai, who saw Fowler's men leaving the slaughter."

Captain Tsawa nodded. "We'll help you avenge them."

The Maskarai tribesman was ready to strike a deal, but not with Captain Tsawa. "I must have Molembe's word. I must see him here."

"Impossible. He's in the city, hunting for the German."

"Then I will speak to his warlord."

Tsawa looked surprised. "Who do you mean?"

"The warrior who Molembe looked to during the battle. The warrior who brought about our capture."

Captain Tsawa suddenly knew who he was talking about. "You mean the American who was with us?"

"The warrior," Zhoave repeated.

"I'll see if I can get him out here," Tsawa said. "It'll take a couple of hours. Perhaps more."

"I will wait for him in the desert. Alone." Then Zhoave gave him the rendezvous point, a dried water hole a mile away from the outpost.

"The warrior will come," Captain Tsawa promised.

He accompanied the Maskarai tribesman back to the gate, then called for his radioman.

A coded message was transmitted to a Serpentine Force chopper, then to Molembe's Intelligence unit in the capital. A short time later the answer came back.

The warlord was on the way.

THE HELICOPTER FLEW straight from Zandeville, touched down at the outpost for a briefing, then lifted off once again and headed for the rendezvous.

After a quick recon of the area satisfied the pilot that he wasn't setting down in the middle of an ambush, he landed on the hard-baked ground in the center of the dead oasis.

Bolan jumped down from the chopper and approached the hooded Maskarai warrior. The two men greeted each other, then began to negotiate.

In return for finding the hostages and leading the ZIS to them, he wanted one thing—he wanted the war to continue until the Desert Knights were pushed out of his land.

Bolan gave him his word, and they began planning for the day when the Maskarai joined the Desert Knights.

FOUR ROWS OF MARINES were doing calisthenics on the deck of the American assault ship when the CH-46 Sea Knight carrying Mack Bolan made its approach.

The aircraft had picked him up five miles out to sea from the deck of one of nearly a dozen yachts dragooned into the ZIS fleet. They were part of Molembe's unofficial navy, piloted by commandos who were unknown to the rank-and-file members of ZIS and, hopefully, to Heinrich Fowler's informants. They'd be waiting for Bolan after he returned from his mid-Atlantic shopping expedition.

As the Sea Knight touched down on the white-circled helipad, Bolan thought how easy it would be to just load the Marines onto the choppers and drop them onto the mountain fortresses.

The four assault ships in the area could carry up to twenty Sea Knights each or a mix of Harrier aircraft and Sea Stallions, enough capability to fight a small war if they got the green light.

The Marines could engage the enemy in strength, dig them out of their strongholds and bring the fighting to a quick end. That would ensure that the acting government had a solid base to operate from in the event that President Sabda never made it back alive.

But the green light wasn't coming. Not yet. Maybe not until it was too late.

Bolan jumped onto the deck, slinging his gear bag over his shoulder. Almost immediately the black-clad warrior was spirited out of sight as Hal Brognola ushered him below decks to a small briefing room that had been commandeered by the Justice operative.

"Welcome to the floating newsroom," Brognola said, closing the door behind him. "You're just in time for the photo spread." The big Fed led him over to a slanting counter that ran around three sides of the room. Several recent satellite photos of the Harana

Desert and the cities on the coast were spread out on the counter.

"All the news that's fit to print?" Bolan said, scanning the photographs and Intelligence summaries.

"All the news that's fit to hide. We've got every square inch of the city covered, and too much desert for my taste."

U.S. reconnaissance satellites and overflights had been tasked to Zandesi hot spots, providing a bird's-eye view of what was going on at ground level. Circles and notations in black marker covered many of the photographs.

High-resolution shots of the Zandeville White House and the buildings surrounding the presidential complex were laid out side by side, revealing the presence of several armed units on the rooftops.

"I hope these men are working for Molembe," Brognola said, tapping a pointer onto several of the pictured units. "Know anything about them?"

"Fits in with Molembe's operations," Bolan said. "He's got some deep-cover operatives stationed all over the capital. They're poised to operate as quick-reaction teams. I'll check it out with him when I get back to make sure these are still his people."

There were also several photos of villas with protected courtyards identified as possible bases for Fowler's confederates in the city.

A number of photos highlighted farms and villas in the outlying area that also showed a lot of activity where people were gathering for safety, many of them with weapons.

"Most places near Z'ville have become armed camps," Brognola said. "They're all waiting for something to come down. Something's definitely in the air, Striker."

"Yeah, I noticed. They're getting ready to shoot first and ask questions later."

Bolan carefully studied the photos of the Zandesian capital, imprinting them in his memory. Though he'd share most of the hard Intel with Molembe, he planned on withholding some of it as a way of testing the ZIS chief's openness about his troop strength and positions.

It was standard procedure. The Executioner believed in trusting his fellow man, as long as he could verify that trust. Little things like that kept a man alive.

He moved on to the photos of the Harana Desert. "Any luck here?" Bolan asked, surveying the world of Zandesi in miniature.

"Oh, yeah," Brognola replied, "we've had lots of luck. We found Fowler's main hideout right here." He smacked the tip of the pointer on a whirlpool of mountain ridges. Then he smacked the pointer on a narrow canyon. "And here."

The pointer moved on again to still another canyon. "And here. The son of a bitch has a small army of men who do nothing but create false trails. Striking camps, setting ambushes, marching to nowhere. Still no sign of where he's keeping President Sabda. The bastard's good, but we'll find his real base sooner or later."

"Sooner, I hope," Bolan said. "That's why I came with a shopping list. If our friends in the desert come through for us, I want to be able to come through for them."

"What do you need?"

"To start with, I want three choppers."

"You don't ask for much."

"We need the replacements to get Serpentine Force back up to snuff. Three Lynx choppers, the army version. That's what Molembe's men are trained on."

"Lynx choppers aren't the flavor of the month, Striker. Maybe you haven't noticed, but the only birds flying from this ship are Sea Knights and Sea Stallions. Not to mention the fact that we can't use them in Zandesi."

"I notice that we got a lot of firepower out here and it's not firing at all," Bolan said.

The American ships still had a heavy presence in the waters of the Atlantic, but the psychological impact was waning. The longer they stayed there the more ineffectual they seemed. Now they were just adrift, waiting until all hell broke loose.

But by then the country itself could be teetering on the brink. According to the insane rules of diplomacy, the U.S. had to refrain from direct military involvement—until the death tolls mounted and Zandesi was ripped apart.

Maybe then the ships would go in and evacuate American citizens and friendlies, whomever they could pluck from the ruins. Another Armageddon in Africa, Bolan thought, picturing the other war-grounds he'd walked through on the continent.

"Like I said," Bolan repeated, "they have to be Lynx choppers so it appears there's no outside help involved. Ask around in the private sector."

"All right, Mack, I'll work on it. See what I can work out with the Brits. They might have something in the area."

Brognola then turned back to the photographs laid out before them. "Now let's go over these again."

Both men pored over the photographs, picking out likely targets for Bolan and the probable targets that would be selected by the Desert Knights.

By the time they were finished, the Executioner had mapped out the next stage of his campaign. It would be a brief tour in hell.

"Okay," Brognola said, "before you clue Molembe in on what the little birds have told us, clue me in on his frame of mind. We all know there's no guarantee we'll get Sabda back in one piece. How's Molembe holding up under all of this pressure?"

"He's a survivor. Molembe lived through Nashonge's regime and he's holding things together now."

"But if Sabda doesn't come back, is Molembe of presidential caliber?"

"He's a good man to have on your side in a firefight. He's more at home in the field than working behind a desk or fighting diplomatic war in a suit."

"I know the type," Brognola said, looking hard at Bolan. "Guys like that can stretch if they have to."

"Right. He's a soldier all the way, but if the country calls upon him, his sense of obligation will keep him at the reins."

"Good. He's still got the confidence of the international community, but that could change quick enough if Fowler unleashes any more of his fatal surprises on the Zandesians.''

"He's capable of it," Bolan said. "So far he's tried pitched battles in the desert and terror attacks in the city. But he hasn't played all of his cards yet. If things go bad for him, there's always a more crippling kind of sabotage."

They went over some of the possible targets Fowler might hit if he escalated the terror. He'd been in control long enough to know the weaker links of Zandesi's infrastructure—power stations, banks, water and food supplies. His targets were limitless.

So far the only thing that kept Fowler in check was his goal of retaking the reins of power. He didn't want to sit on the throne of a country in ruins. But if he reached the point of no return and realized the throne would stay out of his grasp, he just might try to take the country down with him.

"That's where you come in, Striker," Brognola said. "Don't give him the chance."

"And that's where *you* come in. Get us the helicopters, Hal. We need them. Fully equipped gunships, ready to roll."

"You're looking for miracles," Brognola told him.

Bolan nodded, rolling up some of the photographs. The Intel would be transferred to ZIS charts, then the photos would be destroyed. "I'll take whatever you can give me. Miracles *and* machine guns."

IN THE HARSH LIGHT of day, sections of the city resembled a dug-up graveyard. Remnants of stone-walled houses stood like tombstones marking the death of Zandeville.

Death that had come in the night.

The shooting that had begun along the resort strips quickly spread throughout the city. Amid the mad bursts of automatic fire, loud explosions could be heard throughout the night as grenades were tossed randomly inside the homes.

Now the city was an armed camp. Houses were barred and locked. Cars were parked directly in front of doors, both as obstacles to intruders and for quick getaways if the war came to the occupants.

Footsteps outside on the street were matched by furtive sounds from inside the houses as the home owners watched anyone who passed by. Often they watched through cross hairs.

The terror had cut a grisly path through some sections of the city, but left others untouched, as if it were massacre by lottery.

Martin Molembe and his men patrolled through the wreckage of the capital, trying to pick up traces of the marauders and at the same time trying to calm down the inhabitants of the city.

Broken windows littered the streets. Doors torn from their hinges lay flat on the ground like entrances to Hades. And in many cases the bullet-ridden corpses of those killed by the death squads were found in their houses.

The hesitant reports of witnesses were all the same—blue-uniformed men looking for terrorists had burst into houses at random, shot up anything that moved, then went on to their next target.

It was a replay of the revolutions and civil wars that hit so many other countries in Africa. Terrorists would murder civilians, then government troops would come in and murder more civilians, claiming they were terrorists.

Molembe had put out the word that it wasn't government troops who'd committed the murders. Radio and television reports linked the attack to stolen uniforms and an influx of mercenaries into the capital.

But it was hard to believe.

Anyone who encountered the real ZIS teams the day after the slaughter was bound to be spooked at the sight of so many men in uniforms.

Molembe himself was spooked. At the end of the day he was nearly incapable of speech, remembering the dead faces of men he'd known for years, hearing voices from a better time echoing in his head.

When the last ambulance drove off, Molembe climbed into the back of his car and nodded to the driver, who waited for the other armored cars to get in place behind and in front of him, then drove off toward the presidential palace.

Molembe sighed as he glanced back at the ruin. "It can't happen again," he muttered. "They'll try tonight and the next night, but we can't let them beat us. There's only one way to do it...."

His fists clenched instinctively, the sharply etched veins rising prominently on his forearms. "I know what to do."

To the driver who caught his image in the rearview mirror, Molembe looked like a man possessed—or dispossessed.

The statesman had fled. The warrior had taken control.

LATER THAT NIGHT Bolan stood on the rooftop of the presidential palace, scanning the skyline. Two blocks away flares suddenly rained down upon the streets, searing away the blanket of darkness.

Then came the organized roar of a hidden machine-gun nest coming to life. The tripod-mounted SMGs were set up in the upper floors of the buildings surrounding the presidential palace, giving the ZIS gunners control of every inch of the street.

They'd developed a nearly infallible tactic for dealing with the mercenaries prowling the night. The moment any of Fowler's men appeared in the street, the machine gunners opened up with a barrage at their feet. While the spray of lead kicked up tar and concrete, the gunners strafed the road behind them.

With pieces of earth flying all around, the mercs knew in seconds that they were caught in the middle of a trap with steel teeth and were forced immediately to make their choice—fight or flight. But both courses led to a quick and bloody death.

The third alternative was surrender, which held the most promise.

In the face of heavy machine-gun fire, most of Fowler's units threw down their weapons and lifted their hands above their heads, as if they were religiously acknowledging a greater power than them— the greater glory of guns.

The sporadic gunfire had been erupting all night long as small bands of Fowler's men tried to continue their terror raids from the previous night, many of them heading for the presidential palace. Dressed in stolen ZIS uniforms, they'd figured it would be an easy approach.

But they were dead wrong. The ploy had backfired. There was no confusion on the part of the defenders. They opened up on the hardmen without hesitation, almost as if Fowler's men wore signs that broadcast just who they were.

And in a way they did.

Molembe had forbidden his own troops to wear their uniforms and as an added precaution had given strict orders for them not to leave their posts.

That meant anyone moving on the streets wasn't part of the ZIS, and anyone who was in uniform was one of Fowler's men. Their surprise attack had suddenly turned into a suicide assault against impregnable positions.

Though many of the Desert Knights reached their goal of entering the presidential palace, it wasn't in the way they'd imagined. They came in under guard, were taken to the holding cells below ground and interrogated immediately.

Stunned by the rapidity of their capture, the sudden turnaround of events, they were in the right frame of mind to cooperate with the ZIS. Especially since the only remaining choice was for them to be put back out on the street in full uniform and in the bright light of flares.

There would be no coming back a second time.

Faced with certain death, they talked, revealing the locations of the safehouses where they'd changed into the stolen uniforms.

The Intelligence mounted as more and more of Fowler's Desert Knights deserted. A steady parade of hardmen were either taken prisoner or taken out of action permanently if they tried to resist.

Bolan walked in the rooftop breeze as echoes of gunfire drifted over the city. It was the sound of war, a sound the warrior was used to. Perhaps Fowler's troops would be routed, perhaps not. But the bottom line this night was that men would die. And they'd all be one step closer to the final battle.

DOWNSTAIRS IN HIS OFFICE Martin Molembe was dreaming of a free Zandesi. Emil Nashonge was gone, and in his place freedom had been coming. Until Molembe lost it. How foolish to think he could lead the country through all this madness. A better man could have done it.

But no other man had come forward.

It was up to him to bring about the free Zandesi he'd envisioned ever since he was a young man going into the army. For years it had been just a dream, daydreams and pipe dreams in the back of his mind.

But as he worked his way up through the system, first as a soldier, then as a security officer, he'd seen that those feelings were shared by others. There were fellow travelers in the government and in the army, all of them on the long road to freedom, a road that was now blocked by his indecision.

Michael Belasko had offered several courses of action that would take them farther down that road. Courses of action that, once started, would force Fowler's hand. There would be no turning back.

Molembe sat at his desk.

Until now he'd been waiting for others to act. But the American was right. They could no longer wait for the mercenaries to attack and hope they could stop them. Now it was time for them to make a move.

A time for war.

9

Steel-guitar music whined into the night, filtering through the open windows of the off-hours clubs in the Joyhouse District of Zandeville.

With the capture of so many of the mercenaries responsible for the terror, the city had almost returned to normal. And Joyhouse had bounced back in all of its decadent glory.

Bars, bordellos and private clubs flourished side by side on the crowded cobblestoned streets that wound down toward the waterfront in rickety grandeur. The style of buildings was chaotic, looking as if an architect on a binge had worked his way down the streets designing whatever came to mind.

Wild West-style saloons with wraparound balconies stood side by side with modest whitewashed buildings that looked like thousand-year-old monasteries. Two- and three-story buildings with railing-guarded porches leaned toward the street like wooden avalanches.

While many of the buildings were drab, dull affairs, some of them were splashed with heavily detailed murals that depicted the history of the house or highlighted its current offerings, mostly gambling or girls.

The more-profitable ones sported neon signs over their picture windows.

No matter how well they were doing, most of the clubs shared something in common—they were illegal. During the day they were homes or small businesses, but at night they transformed themselves into joy houses.

Authorities seldom bothered them. The Joyhouse District had a long and glorious tradition in Zandeville. Civil war or not, the tradition was hard to break. Though it was a poor cousin to the strip of exclusive clubs glowing like harbor lights along the south end of Zandeville Bay, Joyhouse was the place of choice for most of the locals.

That included Martin Molembe, who led Mack Bolan down a winding street full of slanting clubs that tilted toward the sea. It was shortly past midnight, and their target was a sprawling two-story saloon with loud music and laughter that drifted into the street.

Judging from the crowd, it was the Hilton of after-hours clubs. Several couples sat hunched over small round tables on the wide street-level porch, sharing bottles of wine and making plans for the evening.

A quartet of unattached women in tight tube tops and short skirts leaned over the spindle railing. They looked young but worldly as their shadowed eyes scanned the two approaching men.

"Cops or customers?" said a young woman in a shocking pink top that showed off the impressive contours of her bust.

"Maybe both," the woman next to her replied.

Their laughter floated on a fan-fed breeze of perfume, smoke and sweat.

Bolan and Molembe pushed through the doors and stepped into the comfortable darkness. Several hardmen were sitting at a long wooden bench off to one side of the room. The unofficial doormen turned and watched the newcomers.

A bullnecked man with a gleaming shaved skull sat at the end of the table, a scowl etched on his face. He was obviously in charge of the reception crew. He altered the scowl into a neutral grimace and nodded slightly at Molembe. Then he gave Bolan a cursory glance and looked away.

"Don't tell me," Bolan said. "That was the maître d' and we passed inspection."

Molembe laughed. "His name is Saint-Denis, and he's a lot of things to a lot of people."

"Patron saint of the bar-front bouncers," Bolan suggested, sliding a ladder-back chair across the floor, then sitting at a black-laquered table with a maze of beer rings.

"He *is* the best," Molembe said, dropping into the chair across from Bolan. "When you get bounced by Saint-Denis you don't always get up. Fortunately he's on the right side."

A tanned blonde with a braid of hair reaching halfway down her bare back materialized by the table. Her thin white cotton top was a concoction of wire-thin straps, and had a low-cut bodice that showed a generous expanse of flesh. Her eyes were as blue and as cold as the sea.

They had to be, Bolan realized, to survive in a place like this.

Taking out a pen and pad, she looked down at Molembe. "The usual?" she asked.

"Not tonight. I'll just have a pot of tea. I'm working."

"A shame," she said. "Him, too?"

"Ask him."

"A pleasure." She turned toward Bolan, her eyes flickering with warmth for a moment as she looked at him. Whether it was genuine or just part of her hostess routine, he couldn't tell. "What'll you have?"

"What's available?"

"Ask me again at closing time and we'll see. Right now you can pick your poison." She rattled off a list of beers, whiskeys and exotic drinks.

"Tea sounds fine."

"Sure," she said, raising her eyebrows. "Coming right up. But be careful. It's real strong."

Bolan smiled and watched her glide away through the crowd. "Who is she?"

"She's not part of the decor," Molembe warned. "She's a friend."

"She have a name?"

"Lorraine."

"How does she fit in with all this?"

"She runs this place," Molembe replied, "with a little help from some silent partners." He glanced over at Saint-Denis and his crew.

"Just one big deadly family," Bolan said. "Is this your home away from home?"

"It's one of the safest places I know."

"Relative to what? It looks like a lot of other clip joints I've seen. For the right price you get whatever you want. Drinks, drugs—" the warrior looked around at the available women "—women."

"Drinks, yes. Drugs, no. As far as women go, who knows? That's not my affair. Besides, so far I've seen nothing that makes me suspicious in that regard."

"Right," Bolan said as he watched a bar girl proposition a man just a few feet away from them.

"I have to trust the people," Molembe said, "if I want them to trust me. But I'm serious about this place. Consider it an oasis. In most Joyhouse joints, you need eyes in the back of your head. Here, you just need to mention my name."

"I see. And that gets me a free lunch?"

"Free passage," Molembe insisted. "Remember this place, remember these people. After all, you're the one who wanted to inspect the troops. Those satellite photos don't show everything, you know."

Bolan nodded. The night on the town was business, not pleasure. When Molembe had told him he was ready to go to war, the warrior pressed the ZIS man to show him where his units were stationed so there wouldn't be any deadly surprises.

And at the same time Bolan realized he, too, was being seen and studied by the eyes of an invisible army. It was taking a chance, but it was better to be seen now than to be shot at later.

They'd already made the rounds of several of Molembe's deep-cover strongholds throughout Zandeville. This nightclub was one of the last on the list. And one of the most important. Smack in the middle of the capital, there was little going on that escaped the attention of Molembe's people.

After Lorraine reappeared with the tea and a rather large bill, Molembe pointed toward the corner of the room where someone was pulling the plug from the jukebox.

The jukebox fell silent as a group of musicians climbed up onto a small raised platform covered with instruments. Emblazoned on the head of the drum in red letters was the name of the band, Joyhouse Arkestra.

"Take a good look at them," Molembe said.

There were four men and a woman in the band. The man closest to the front of the stage wore a loose-fitting white shirt that hung down to his knees. It gave him a monkish look at first, but the look was banished the moment he picked up the double-necked bass guitar and smiled down at the audience.

His fingers flew down the bass neck with a mind of their own, tapping out a murky blues number. While the bass notes still hung heavy in the air, his fingers jumped up to the guitar neck and strummed a few jangling chords.

One by one the others joined in, and the wandering notes gradually found each other in a mix of African and Caribbean rhythms. The woman started chanting, gradually escalating her voice to belt out sweet tropical blues.

Life went on, Bolan reminded himself. No matter what happened, the party continued.

Like the others he found himself caught by the soulful voice. But unlike the others he pulled himself away from it quickly, studying the faces of the band members and the men in Saint-Denis's crew.

"Let's take a walk," Molembe suggested. He got up and led Bolan in front of the stage. The musicians casually followed their movements as they passed by.

Molembe then worked his way through the crowd and discreetly opened a door that led down a narrow hallway. Midway down the corridor on the left side was a closed door with a sign printed in official-looking block letters: Unauthorized Persons Will Never Be Seen Again—The Management.

"Nice friendly touch," Bolan observed.

"Yes," Molembe grunted, "the management's a real bitch here." Then, as if there was any lingering doubt about who managed the club, Molembe fished a set of keys from his pocket and opened the door.

It looked like a dressing room at first. Hanging from several hooks on the wall were an assortment of open-necked robes, log-splashed T-shirts and faded jeans. Leaning against the wall were several wide instrument cases.

"What gives?" Bolan asked. "Are we auditioning?"

"All part of the tour," Molembe replied. "Just taking inventory." Then he grabbed one of the guitar cases and flipped it on top of a tall wooden dresser with a heavy thud. He opened the clasps and turned back the lid.

Inside the case were three Heckler & Koch MP-5 SD submachine guns. As well as a sound suppressor, each SMG was equipped with a laser-lock sighting system for instant target acquisition. The laser beam would pinpoint exactly where the burst was going to hit.

Molembe opened another case, revealing short-barreled submachine guns. The MP-5 Kurz models were nearly one foot shorter than the SD model and had an extra pole grip just beneath the barrel for maximum control when it was fired.

"Nice instruments," Bolan said. "These guys know how to play them?"

"Those men are professionals. Onstage and off."

Bolan nodded. "You're saying that I can count on the band."

"If you find yourself in the thick of it, you can always count on them to play a tune for you," Molembe said, a touch of pride in his voice, and Bolan knew he'd brought this unit along carefully. "That's one orchestra that knows how to rock."

Molembe flipped the case shut, replaced it with the others, then led Bolan out of the room.

"Let's finish our tour," the security chief suggested. "It's going to be a long night. In a little while we're going to do some midnight banking at the treasury."

THE BANK OF ZANDESI was emptied in the middle of the night. Or so it seemed to anyone watching from the shadows. Despite the late hour, people *were* watching. The ZIS had carefully leaked details about the "secret" move of treasury bullion to suspected informants, guaranteeing that some of Fowler's people would observe the clandestine transfer.

Unmarked ZIS cars were parked on both sides of the street, engines running. Every car had a driver and a man running shotgun.

Martin Molembe personally supervised the operation from inside the bank vault.

The Executioner made himself visible with the street detail, conferring with the drivers and now and then scanning the streets—intentionally overlooking the infiltrators who'd come to watch the transfer.

Fowler had sent sympathizers, not soldiers, who eagerly gathered the disinformation. Had they been assassins and tried to eliminate Bolan or Molembe, they'd have been immediately taken out by hidden rooftop sniper units on both sides of the street.

It was a very quick and professional operation.

The transfer units came rolling down the street in snub-nosed armored vans. They pulled up in front of the thick glass doors of the bank and angled the vehicles so the back doors faced the main entrance. Uniformed guards hopped from the back of the vehicles and hurried up the stairs.

A string of ZIS officers stood with their weapons at the ready, protecting them every step of the way. Similarly armed men lined the way inside the bank to the open vault.

Then the apparent exodus of treasure began. Bullion-laden carts were wheeled down the stairs and raised into the back of the vans.

An elite commando unit specially selected for the assignment followed the vans in black bulletproof cars. The unusual measure reinforced the cover, especially since the unit was drawn from Serpentine Force chopper pilots who normally hunted down the Desert Knights.

Riding in the middle car of the Serpentine Force bodyguard was Julian, the pilot suspected of collaborating with Fowler. His copilot was beside him. Both men were given a front-row view of the vans delivering their cargo to its new location, which was a brick museum that had once been a fort guarding the mouth of the harbor.

Thanks to his informants in Serpentine Force, Fowler would be one of the first to know of the bullion's new location.

Molembe and Bolan had decided it was the best way of using the men. Rather than throwing them into jail, the two pilots had been cut out of the real desert operations and assigned patrol missions that kept them out of the way. But tonight they were completing their real assignment—betraying their country.

Intelligence had indicated that Fowler's contingency plan involved the looting of the treasury. If he couldn't steal the country, he'd steal the country's fortune.

And here the ZIS was giving it to him on a golden platter. All he had to do now was to try to take it. But if the man managed to fight his way in, the only thing he'd capture would be gold-painted iron bars.

10

Shadows moved in the darkness as the blacksuited shock troops moved toward the edge of the wooded ridge. While the snipers took up positions along the tree line, a three-man unit bearing wire cutters crawled downhill toward the high wire fence that bordered the eastern perimeter of the Zandeville Export Company, one of the largest corporations in the Zandesian capital.

At night the compound resembled a small sleeping city, with isolated streetlights lighting the intersections of the long roads that ran along the huge hangar-shaped warehouses and smaller administrative buildings.

Railroad tracks lined the full length of many of the warehouses. Perched on the tracks opposite the loading docks were dully painted dust-covered railcars. Some of the cars were wide open, but others had their doors closed, barred and sealed. At both ends of the buildings stood tall corrugated doors with canvas-covered wooden bumpers for the trucks to back up against.

During the day the export company thrived, full of the hubbub of commerce as the company conducted a solid business. Though it should have been an attractive target for looters, none of the troubles afflicting the rest of the capital touched down at the export company.

During the riots people stayed away from the fenced-in compound. It was almost as if the company led a charmed existence—or more appropriately a cursed one. The average Zandesian was wary of the place.

It was haunted with the presence of Heinrich Fowler.

Despite the paper trail that hid the real ownership of the company, it was fairly obvious that it was controlled by the would-be leader of Zandesi. Men who were close to Fowler during Nashonge's reign still operated the company.

The ownership of ZEC was an open secret, and the locals didn't mind. They kept working and drawing their pay, safe in the knowledge that the export company was one of the safest places to be. And they were right—at least during daytime hours.

But at night the firm exported a more expensive commodity. Murder.

Satellite photos had revealed a buildup of "night shift" workers inside the gates, though the company never operated at night. Molembe's men had watched the place closely, noting the comings and goings of hard-looking men who didn't make their money loading trucks and railcar containers from the warehouse bays.

By shadowing the night shift, the ZIS surveillance teams were led to other safehouses in the capital, many of them already highlighted on the satellite photos as probable sites for Fowler's city legion.

The first terror attack had been just a taste of what was to come. Fowler had sent out the call to his people in the capital. They were gathering behind the gates of the export company and in nearby safehouses, getting ready to make their move.

The ZIS was going to make theirs first.

The preemptive strike began slowly, almost casually, as several unmarked ZIS cars drove down the streets leading to the access gates of the export company. Blue-uniformed ZIS officers filtered from the dark cars and took up positions at the end of the streets where they could watch the gates without being seen.

Then one official ZIS car rolled up to the main gate on the north side of the complex. Officers stepped out of the vehicle and began shining flashlights through the wires, calling for someone to come open the gate.

The shock troops watched from the distant ridge. With them was Mack Bolan.

Webs of moonlight filtered through the branches above the blacksuited, black-faced Executioner as the inland breeze swept through the forested ridge.

Sitting in a tree-shrouded pocket of darkness, the warrior scanned the inside of the compound with the thermal imager. The night-vision device showed several ghostly figures emerging from unlit doorways. They stood on stairwells, along warehouse loading docks, behind half-opened windows, alerted by the noise at the gate.

All of them were heavily armed.

The men closest to the brightly lit front gate had their weapons aimed at the four ZIS officers who were still shouting for someone to come to the gate before they were forced to smash it down.

The gate house was dark and empty, but fifty feet inside the gate there was activity at a small office that sat close to the main road. A glare of light suddenly cut through the darkness as a door slammed open.

Cursing loudly, a man wearing a dark necktie and a white shirt with rolled-up sleeves thumped down the steps and headed toward the gate.

At first glance he looked like a man who'd stayed late to go over the books or finish some paperwork. Obviously a man impatient with interruptions, he kicked some loose gravel out of the roadbed as he stalked closer to the gate.

It was a very convincing portrait—except for the automatic holstered in the belt at the small of his back. Except for the surveillance photos that had identified him as Gunther Braun, a mercenary whose record of atrocities had put a price on his head on the East African coast.

A former associate of Heinrich Fowler's, he'd answered his friend's call for reinforcements. Braun and several of his men had been ushered into the compound hidden inside railcars.

A lot of matériel had also found its way into the warehouses via the railcars. Surveillance photos showed special crews overseeing the off-loading of a number of cars, carefully stowing their crates in separate bays. Molembe's contacts in the day-shift work force had told him of the special areas reserved for some of the incoming freight.

Bolan studied the warehouses again, getting a solid picture in his mind of the layout.

Then he trained the night-vision device on Braun's four-man backup unit, which was quietly slipping out a side door on the dark side of the office building.

Unseen by the ZIS officers at the gate—but expected by Molembe's sniper crew, who followed them through their own night scopes—the hardmen crept along the side of the building, keeping in the shadows.

The white-shirted hatchet man started talking through the fence with the ZIS officers to cover up any sounds his backup team might be making.

"Take a look," Bolan said, passing the binocular-sized thermal imager back to Molembe, who'd been crouching next to him on the ridge. "Over there." He pointed toward the gun-wielding quartet. "Must be a midnight housekeeping crew."

Molembe swept the imager over the office building, then studied the other rifle teams spread out throughout the interior of the compound. "Working overtime in a war zone. Hope they're getting danger pay."

"Whatever it is, they're earning their keep," Bolan said. "I'd say we found our rioters and saboteurs. Half of Fowler's free-lancers are holed up in there."

"Looks like our Intelligence is right on the money."

"Checks out on all sides," Bolan said. "Satellite photos, your own surveillance teams *and* the Intel from Nicholas Croy point to this place as Fowler's main staging area."

"Photographs I can believe," Molembe said softly. "My own people I can believe. But Croy is the worst sort of criminal. I trust him like I'd trust the devil."

"Croy was fairly high up in Fowler's crew from the beginning. So far everything he's told us has come to pass."

Molembe didn't deny it. Just as Croy had predicted, Fowler tried to force negotiations by keeping Sabda hidden and Molembe's troops occupied in the desert. Failing that, he shifted attention to Zandeville. Then came the riots and the terror attacks. All of it was part of a carefully orchestrated campaign that was rushing toward a final stage of all-out warfare.

Bolan looked down at the compound full of men carrying submachine guns and automatic rifles. "My guess is we're about nine millimeters away from the final stage."

"Maybe Croy's telling the truth," Molembe said. "Maybe he's painted it with his lies. We'll know soon enough."

While they waited for the ZIS officers to set up their diversion, Bolan thought back to the conversations he'd had with the Australian hardman. According to the gospel of Nick Croy, President Sabda would only be kept alive as long as he could provide leverage for Fowler's position. Once Fowler gave the go-ahead to the final stage, Sabda's life expectancy would be very short indeed.

While his mercenary troops plunged Zandesi into chaos, Fowler would move toward his ultimate target, the National Bank of Zandesi. If he couldn't take over the government, he'd steal what propped up that government—the gold bullion reserves in the national treasury.

He'd leave behind a bankrupt country.

Knowing what Fowler was planning was one thing. Stopping him was another. It was a risky operation that could blow up in their faces.

Though the majority of the profits of the Zandeville Export Company went to Fowler's silent partners, a number of foreign shareholders owned the rest of the company stock. Legitimate French, U.S., Dutch and German businessmen had used their contacts to give the company an international presence.

It was a showcase for Zandesian enterprise.

If the operation went wrong, the showcase would come crashing down around them. Molembe and the ZIS would be discredited in the eyes of the world. They might win the battle and lose the throne.

"You still want to go in there alone?" Molembe asked.

"That's the best way," Bolan replied. "If I'm in there by myself, I'll know who the enemy is—everyone inside the fence. If we go in with force, it'll be a free-for-all. Let's stick to what we planned. Wait until all hell breaks loose, then go in. I'll be done and gone by then. Or dead and gone."

THROUGH THE WIRE GATE the senior ZIS officer shone his flashlight on Gunther Braun, casting a Halloweenish glint onto the hardman's angular face.

"All right," Braun snapped, shielding his eyes with his hand. "I'm willing to talk things over."

"Thank you for cooperating," the officer said, ceremoniously holstering the automatic he'd drawn a moment earlier. It had achieved its desired effect, silencing his blustering protest about police harassment. He lowered the flashlight beam to the ground.

"As I was saying," the officer continued, "we're looking for an armed man we've tracked through this neighborhood. We believe he's one of the saboteurs plaguing our city. If so, he's a most dangerous man."

"Not to us," Braun replied. "Believe me, we damned well know how to look after ourselves in here."

The officer glanced around the inside of the compound as if he could see the armed mercs hiding in the darkness. "Perhaps you can take care of yourselves," he agreed, "but even so, if you do find an intruder, let us know first—before you take care of him."

Braun nodded and started backing away from the gate.

Just then another ZIS car pulled up, its bubble-top lights flickering all along the fence and riveting the attention of every gunman inside the compound.

The car stopped near the senior officer, and one of the uniformed men stepped out of the vehicle. He spoke rapidly with him, then climbed back into his car and drove off.

"We've got him," the officer said to Braun. "Thanks for your help."

"Anytime," Braun responded in a sour voice. But as he walked back toward the office building, he couldn't help smiling, thinking of the poor innocent bastard just picked up by the ZIS. "Better him than us," he muttered.

ON THE EASTERN SIDE of the compound, Mack Bolan went into action as soon as the lights of the ZIS car diverted the attention of the mercenary night workers.

He pulled back the fence where the wire cutters had done their job, then slipped his satchel onto the grass on the other side. He climbed through, then slowly released his grip on the fence, replacing the chain links.

Bolan studied the ridge beyond the fence, fixing it into his memory. He'd have to pass this way again to get out. He picked up the satchel and headed down-hill to a long line of railcars.

He reached the middle of the cars, far away from the lights at the end of the buildings, then scrambled across the splintered tracks, heavy with the scent of oil, rust and rotting wood.

The clearance between railcar and clock was about two feet. Carefully placing his hand on the crumbling concrete dock, he pulled himself up and sprinted to the side of the building. There under the eaves he was swallowed in shadow.

He worked his way down the dock until he came to one of the fire doors. He passed up the first one. It was newly painted, and there was fresh mason work around the lock and hinge.

The warrior kept going until he reached a door with faded red paint. Just as Molembe's contacts on the dayshift had promised, the doorknob and lock were new, but the hinged side of the door was in poor shape.

Bolan reached into a side pocket of his combat vest and removed a sharp spear-point pick that unfolded from a rubber-coated handgrip. He punched the pick into the crumbling concrete, then twisted sharply. Bits of brick and corroded masonry tumbled to the ground. With another push of his hand he widened the gap. More broken brick and rubble rained down onto the dock. In half a minute he removed enough concrete from around the hinges to pull them out of the wall. Opening the door from the hinge side, he slipped into the dark cavernous warehouse.

It wasn't totally black. Light spilled from an office at the end of the warehouse, and slabs of moonlight filtered through the oval windows at the top of the warehouse. Some of the light was blocked by towering stacks of cartons on wooden pallets that reached up to the ceiling, but Bolan had enough light to see where he was going.

He waited until his eyes were adjusted to the darkness, then, staying close to the wall, he headed toward the office. As he neared, he heard snatches of voices and tinny music playing from a radio.

The mercenaries were returning to their posts now that the alert was over.

And they were returning to their card game. The sound of curses and laughter came from the room as the warrior approached. One man raised his opponent, who cursed his ancestors, his creator and every bloody night he'd signed up to stay in Zandesi. And then he tossed in his ante.

Bolan knew the type. Card-carrying, card-playing mercs killing time between killing people.

The Executioner moved away from the wall and worked his way down the rows, sliding between the tall stacks of freight until he could get a closer look at the men in the room.

They were armed to the teeth, automatic rifles and subguns lining the walls.

Most of the men were sitting around a huge gray metal desk that was covered with cards, ashtrays and bottles.

There were seven men in the room, guards whose main job was to protect the matériel that had been so carefully smuggled into the warehouse. And in their eyes they were doing a good job of it. Since the complex was packed with other hardmen just like them in other offices, they couldn't imagine the place being infiltrated by one man.

An army they'd expect. But a lone intruder? Out of the question.

The lone intruder listened a bit more, then moved away from the lighted office toward a forklift area on the left-hand corner of the bay. Yellow slots marked off spaces on the floor for a number of different-sized fork and barrel-clamp lifts parked side by side.

Bolan studied the propane tanks perched atop the back of the lifts, stepped softly to the forklift closest to the wall and unthreaded the fuel hose from the tank. Then he slowly turned the gas-control knob until he heard a small hiss of released pressure.

A cold mist of gas sprayed into the air.

The Executioner moved down the row of lifts, repeating the maneuver several times.

Then he melted back into the darkness.

Bolan made his way to the opposite end of the warehouse, searching for the recently constructed room described by Molembe's informants. The room was guarded during the day by two men who supervised the special crews.

He found what he was looking for in the second-to-last bay. Plywood walls reaching halfway to the ceiling cordoned off one side of the bay from the rest of the storage areas. The makeshift room had an opening large enough and wide enough to accommodate the booms of the forklifts that moved freight in and out.

Two of the forklifts had been left inside the room. One of them was parked in the corner while another sat close to the entrance. Its heavy, flat tines rested on the floor, still holding a stack of long, heavy wooden crates raised three feet above the ground.

The room was divided into two sections, one with cardboard cartons stacked on wooden pallets, and one with wooden crates piled on top of one another.

Like a doctor making house calls, Bolan stepped inside the room and set down the satchel. This was the operating room, and soon it would be time for radical surgery.

He sprinted to the forklift. Taking out his pick, he pried off the lid of the top crate and shone the light of the small palm-sized flashlight inside.

The oval beam revealed a crate full of AK-47s, and a quick inspection of several other crates revealed a large cache of the Soviet-made weapons.

Moving to another row and prying open more crates, Bolan discovered RPG-7V rocket launchers and cases of muzzle-loaded rocket charges. The HEAT rounds could knock out armored vehicles and bunkers, and no doubt were brought in to use against the ZIS machine-gun emplacements throughout the city.

The Executioner went over to one of the cardboard-covered pallets and tested the weight of one of the cartons. He hoisted it over his shoulder, then set it quietly on top of the crates on the forklift.

He made a few quick slashes with his knife, then raised the jagged lid to see the blue uniforms of the ZIS. This was where Fowler had outfitted his counterfeit ZIS death squads.

Then the warrior opened his satchel and took out adhesive-backed strips of C-4 plastic explosive, affixed them to the crates, wired them and set the timer prepared by Molembe's technical crew.

He gave himself five minutes to get out.

Bolan backed out of the room quietly and headed for the western side of the warehouse—then froze as a clicking sound echoed down the bay.

Several switches were flicked on simultaneously as a bank of overhead lights flooded the bay with light.

Bolan was caught dead in the open.

He looked over his shoulder and saw one of the former cardplayers staring back at him, open-mouthed and speechless—until his training took over.

The man shouted an alarm and reached for his side arm.

The Executioner yanked the silenced Beretta free of the Velcro harness on his chest as his eyes searched for the man's heart. There was no time to aim, only time for gut reaction.

The merc's automatic cleared leather, the arc of the barrel rising as the gunman went by *his* instincts.

The silenced 3-round burst that flew from Bolan's weapon appeared to have no effect on the man. At first. But then he jerked back like a swan about to take flight, his arms flapping at his sides.

He took three steps backward before collapsing on the floor, his automatic clattering beside him.

Was the man alone, checking out the armory bay on a whim?

A voice called out in French.

The man's partner was coming from the right side of the warehouse. Still in the next bay, he sounded calm at first. But when there was no response, his voice grew louder. The man swore and called out his partner's name one last time.

"Gilles!"

Bolan muffled his voice and said a few words in French.

The man laughed and swore at Gilles for almost getting himself shot by not responding sooner. Then, gun in hand, he walked around a stack of pallets, stopping dead when he saw the Executioner.

"So long," Bolan said, firing off a 3-round burst.

But the newcomer had thrown himself out of the way at the last moment. The bullets struck him in the left shoulder and flung him to the ground, but he managed to hold on to his weapon and squeeze off a shot.

The crack of gunfire echoed through the bays as the man pulled the trigger repeatedly, firing wildly in Bolan's direction. The bullets drilled into the walls and crashed through one of the skylights. The gunner seemed more interested in making noise then in nailing Bolan, yelling to his comrades that they were under attack.

Answering shouts erupted from the far end of the warehouse as the hardmen poured out of the office.

Their loud, confused voices suddenly dropped off as they gathered their wits and planned a course of action.

Bolan knew how it would go down. They had the manpower and they had the time. The mercenaries would move bay by bay until they had him cornered.

Simple for them, fatal for Bolan.

At the moment there were too many of them for him to stay and fight it out—especially since reinforcements could surround the warehouse—and too many of them to evade.

He had to even the odds.

A quick burst from the Beretta shattered most of the overhead lights, sending a hard rain of popping glass onto the stacks.

Then the warrior raced back into the makeshift shelter, acutely aware of the numbers ticking down to Doomsday.

He picked up an RPG-7V and a torpedo-shaped rocket, and, pushing the spring-loaded fins of the HEAT rocket into the launcher tube, he returned to the warehouse.

When he reached the aisle where the dead man lay, he knelt, steadied the rocket launcher on his shoulder and sighted at the far end of the warehouse where several men were grouped around the forklifts.

Half of the search party was about to go after him.

To save them the trouble, the Executioner fired the rocket. The warhead shot straight at its target, detonating against the brick wall behind the lifts and showering the area with fast-flying rubble.

The thunderous explosion ignited the propane Bolan had leaked from the tanks, propelling a shock wave down the corridor.

The airborne mercs didn't have a chance as the molten blast punched them onto the concrete floor and kicked them into the afterlife.

Bolan didn't waste time congratulating himself. Even now the other half of the search party would be sealing off the exits while they waited for reinforcements.

The Executioner decided it was time to make his own exit.

Slapping a fresh clip into the Beretta on the run, he returned to the armory, hopped onto the forklift and turned the ignition key. While he shifted the lift into reverse, he pulled the lever to the right of the steering wheel and tilted the boom backward. Then, still carrying the load of crates and cardboard, he raised the forks off the floor.

Bolan wheeled out of the armory room in reverse and backed up all the way to the corridor. Shifting into forward gear, he stomped on the gas pedal and careered into the last bay.

As the forklift rattled and revved, Bolan moved on autopilot, trusting his memory of the layout to get him out. He remembered there was a huge corrugated door at the end of the warehouse, but it was on the eastern side of the building, where the rest of the search party was located.

Still, he had no choice—the bullets whining overhead drilled that point home.

When he reached the last row, the Executioner spun the steering wheel to the left, racing for the eastern side of the warehouse. As the forklift barreled down the row, Bolan pulled up on the lever and raised the wooden crates until they shielded him at eye level.

He took the corner on two wheels, and as the forklift touched down again, he wheeled right and fired left, unloading 3-round bursts at his pursuers. The enemy dived for cover, giving him a few precious seconds.

The end of the warehouse was just ten feet away.

The forks speared the corrugated-metal door a split second before the wooden crates added their mass to the crash. Then the huge forklift barreled through.

The hardmen raced to the wrecked doorway and opened up with everything they had.

Bolan came up firing. He'd jumped off the lift at the last moment, rolling on his shoulders into the darkness. Now he was right beside them, the Beretta 93-R spitting flame.

He swept the doorway with rapid bursts, lifting the mercs into a bloody dance of death that eventually punched them to the ground.

The warrior dived over the low, slanting wall of an access ramp that led up to the outside dock. A split second later a pair of headlights stabbed the air.

Tires screeched and car doors slammed.

Gunther Braun leaped from his car and scanned the dead hardmen.

More cars pulled up as reinforcements arrived. Still in his shirt and tie, like an executive gone berserk, Braun ran from man to man bellowing orders.

He sent most of his forces into the breached door, while he stayed outside and waited for their report. Two of his men were sent down to the outside dock, creeping in the shadows formed by a line of railcars.

Their quarry watched from the ridge as he slowly backed away toward the fence where he'd infiltrated the compound.

Then he sat back to watch the fireworks.

It wasn't long in coming.

Volcanic fire mushroomed into the sky as the blast took off the roof of the warehouse, which exploded in a thunderous spray of wood, metal, concrete and human flesh.

The detonated C-4 took out the armory and a good part of Fowler's army at the same time, casting a fiery glow above the shattered building.

Sirens split the night as Molembe's ZIS units came in on cue. Fire engines, police cars and truckloads of ZIS commandos raced toward the gates, smashing through the barriers.

The surviving hardmen were subdued without resistance.

When the compound was secure, Molembe brought in one of his most formidable weapons—a video crew.

Sweeping through the compound, the cameramen recorded the stolen uniforms scattered on the ground, the weapons spilled from their cases and the large number of slain mercenaries.

"Over here!" Molembe shouted, drawing the attention of one of the cameramen.

The cameraman approached one side of the warehouse where Molembe had positioned Gunther Braun. The captured mercenary was standing in front of a brick wall.

"Tape this," Molembe ordered.

The cameraman warily approached, the video camera resting on his shoulder. "An execution?"

"No, a confession. He has much to say to us." Molembe's eyes hardened as he stared at the mercenary. "Unless you've changed your mind?"

Braun shook his head. "I'm most grateful for your offer of leniency."

"That's good," Molembe said. "Because it's a limited offer. Good for the next ten seconds only."

The merc nodded. Then he began to say the magic words. "My name is Gunther Braun. I'm a mercenary in the employ of Heinrich Fowler. I was smuggling weapons in to the export company to complement Fowler's store of stolen government uniforms. His plan was to unleash a counterfeit army on the capital..."

After Braun was finished, several other captured mercenaries said their piece in front of the cameras. They, too, were talkative, aware that their stay in Zandesi would be cut short in a most unpleasant way unless they told the truth.

That was the danger in relying on mercenaries. When all seemed lost, they were quick to jump to the winning side. Not that Molembe was complaining.

The operation was a success. Rather than risk losing a lot of men in a direct assault on the warehouse complex, they'd done it without a single fatality.

The mercenaries had been attacked from the inside. And by one of their own kind, Molembe thought. No, he amended, by one of ours.

11

Hoofbeats thundered over the cold, hard ground as the Maskarai warriors rode into the night-shadowed camp of Fowler's Desert Knights.

It was at a cul-de-sac in one of the endlessly ribboning canyons that lined Mont Bataille.

Slivers of candlelight flickered from the mouths of caves as some of the mercenaries pushed back the dark blankets hanging over the entrances to watch the return of the tribesmen.

Several more hardmen sat around drinking or sleeping inside the caves that honeycombed the walls of the canyon. They were relaxed and off guard for a simple reason.

In recent nights the Maskarai warriors had assumed a greater role in scouting for the enemy and defending the camp against surprise attack.

With so many of Fowler's men assigned to operations in Zandeville, the desert mercs welcomed the tribesmen who were willing to take on the more dangerous assignments while they savored the luxuries of their cliffside lairs.

To the hardmen it was an ideal situation. ZIS patrols were always on the move, checking out canyon after canyon. And thanks to the Maskarai warriors, the Desert Knights were always one move ahead of them.

The sound of hoofbeats was reassuring.

At first.

But then the hoofbeats increased in volume as the riders galloped into the jagged oval enclosure. The chorus of snorting and shrieking horses grew louder than usual as the animals sensed something in the air.

More riders were returning than had gone out with the war party.

One of the mercenaries finally realized something was wrong as he looked down from the mouth of a cave at the huge number of milling shadows twenty feet below him.

Then he realized the Maskarai weren't there to protect them, but to destroy them. He shouted an alarm and drew his weapon.

A cloaked rider directly below him fired three bursts from a silenced weapon.

Looking upward for a moment, chest and chin whacked by the burst, the merc staggered back against the cliff side. He then slipped forward and dropped to the ground, his death cry swallowed by the sound of the riders as they spread out along the cul-de-sac.

Bolan holstered the Beretta, uncoiled a black nylon rope and whirled a three-pronged grappling hook over his head. When it picked up sufficient speed he let it fly up to the cave.

The high arc of the hook brought it down onto the mouth of the cave where it speared into a jutting lip of rock. Bolan tugged hard to make sure it would hold his weight, then jumped free from his mount.

Two other riders followed suit. Like Bolan, the ZIS commandos were dressed in the desert garb of the Maskarai, and they clambered up to the cave a few seconds behind him.

By then the Executioner was inside, the business end of the Beretta probing the way.

A hardman who'd just been snatched from sleep rushed into the corridor.

Without breaking stride, Bolan triggered a round that kicked the man back into the arms of Morpheus. This time permanently.

A flood of ZIS officers swept inside the cave, some of them spearing the darkness with wide flashlight beams while the others covered their approach.

Gunfire echoed from all around the canyon as mercenaries in adjacent caves awoke to find their former allies at their throats, repaying them for their treachery.

From deep inside Bolan's cave came a chorus of panicked cries, the voices of the hostages, enraged that they'd survived so much only to face death at the hands of their captors.

The mercenary responsible for their confinement and, if necessary, their deaths, raced into the splinter cave, braced himself against the wall to cover all the prisoners, then steadied his submachine gun.

A burst of 9 mm Parabellums threw him off his feet. His trigger finger closed as he fell, studding the dirt with an automatic burst while his own blood spattered down on his body.

Bolan and his commandos filtered into the dark recesses of the splinter cave and found the group of human scarecrows, gaunt from fear and brutality, and minimal food and water. But in their eyes he saw a fire that hadn't gone out.

One by one the hostages stepped forward.

A woman with a tear-streaked face was talking softly to herself in an amazed girlish tone.

A man walked forward with bruises covering his face and his arms. He limped slowly and painfully.

Then another hostage stepped forward, thanking them in a cracked and dry voice. It was Leopold Sabda.

The president of Zandesi stepped in front of the other hostages and, in a voice that had never let go of its authority, said, "Who are you?"

"An adviser," Bolan replied. "And my advice to you and everyone else, Mr. President, is to haul ass out of here."

"But who are you with?"

"I'm with Martin Molembe, Mr. President. And with you."

Sabda stood there like a man who'd just woken up and somehow managed to carry part of his dream with him. All this time he'd dreamed of the moment when he'd be free. But in the back of his mind he'd resigned himself to dying in a dark and forsaken cave.

"You're all free now," Bolan said. "If you want to stay that way, follow me. Those of you who know how to use a weapon, take one of these."

He pointed toward a ZIS man who'd gathered submachine guns and automatic rifles from the fallen mercs and leaned them against a wall of the cave.

Like a man who'd found a golden grail, Stephen Ward limped forward and picked up an AK-47 with a 30-round clip. Bolan watched the man check over the weapon. According to the Maskarai warriors who'd pinpointed the cave where the hostages were held, Ward was the one who'd received the brunt of his captors' brutality. Physically the man was a wreck, but mentally he was primed for battle.

A second man stepped forward. He was a stocky security man at home with the weapons. He picked up one of the SMGs, slung the strap over his shoulder, then tucked it under his arm.

"Anyone else know how to use a weapon?" Bolan asked, looking at the small gathering. "If you're not sure, this isn't the time to start. We don't want you shooting our own people. But if you know how, we can use every man here."

Sabda stepped forward and stared at the weapons. "It's been a long time since I've held one," he said. "Too long." Then he picked up an AK-47. "Now it's time to cast my vote...against Heinrich Fowler."

Bolan gave the former hostages a quick briefing about how the Maskarai had worked with the mercenaries only long enough to set up the attack and had really formed an alliance with the ZIS. "Make sure you know your target before you fire. The Maskarai are on our side. But be ready to fight your way past anyone else."

The networks of caves were linked in many places, intersecting at odd and hidden angles where hardmen could set up an ambush.

"All right," Bolan said, "let's move."

The group of ZIS commandos and Sabda's battered cabinet members hurried back to the main cavern, heading for the entrance.

When they were halfway there they heard a loud clatter behind them. A ragged band of mercenaries emerged from one of the secondary caverns, their weapons clacking together as they tried to regain their balance and get into a shooting position.

Then a deafening barrage stopped them in their tracks. Crouching in a crevice with his AK-47 emptying into the mercs, Stephen Ward shouted a war cry that echoed up and down the cave. It was the cry of freedom found once again after it had been ripped away.

Beside him Leopold Sabda and a ZIS commando opened up at the same time. They'd been leapfrogging through the cave, one group covering the other in turns.

The technique worked perfectly. The pursuing mercs hadn't expected much resistance—they were used to dealing with scared prisoners.

But now they paid for it with their lives.

Their faces froze in surprise as bullets riveted them to the curved, craggy stone corridor. Then they fell forward, leaving strains of red dripping down the rock.

A few moments later the hostages and the rescue team reached the edge of the cave. Depending on their condition, they climbed down the rocky face of the cliff side or slid down the ropes the ZIS commandos had staked into the ground.

Down in the canyon bed, the Maskarai horsemen were circling the cul-de-sac, firing up into the open caves. Ricochets sang against rock now and then, but more often the single shots found human targets. And each time one less merc served in Heinrich Fowler's outlaw army.

When the hostages were put on horseback, the ZIS commandos escorted them out of the canyon. Behind them came Bolan and the Maskarai, carrying their wounded with them.

The horsemen rode hard for a half mile, their cloaks flapping behind them, the moonlight casting their shadows on the desert floor.

They gathered at a temporary base protected by a wall of moonlike spires, where Bolan radioed Serpentine Force, who'd set up their forward operating base just a few miles away in the desert.

Within minutes the steady whir of rotor blades beat the air, growing louder as the pack of gunships bore down on the canyons. There were nine aircraft in action, including three new arrivals, courtesy of Hal Brognola's behind-the-scenes connections.

Now that the hostages were safe, the gunships could go in full blast.

The lead chopper soared through the canyon, announcing its presence with two high-explosive rockets that shattered the face of the cliff. Huge slabs of rock slid to the bottom of the canyon in a thunderous avalanche.

One after the other, the choppers streaked through the canyon, unleashing salvos of high explosives and antipersonnel darts. Metal shredded the air and chopped into the caves, streaming waves of fire scorching the interiors.

The echo from the rockets and the chatter of machine guns merged into a steady roar as bright clouds of flame and smoke settled over the canyon.

There was no escape. After the helicopter assault sealed off the cave mouths, ZIS armored units rolled into the area. The ground troops scanned the canyons with night-vision devices, mopping up when necessary.

The desert network was smashed.

12

"It looks just like the Alamo," Bolan commented, watching the stone face of the darkened fortress museum on the northern edge of Zandeville Bay. "Let's hope we're on the right side this time."

" 'Remember the Alamo,' " Molembe said.

"You know the story?"

"You're not the only student of war, my friend. All of us have learned it firsthand in Zandesi."

"Good," Bolan said, "because the final exam's going to start any minute."

Molembe grunted, growing impatient. Like Bolan, he'd sat in the darkness for hours, peering through palm fronds and brush at the museum.

All around him ZIS commandos did the same.

Molembe's nightfighters were dressed in dark blue fatigues and blue berets. Among them were several Joyhouse irregulars who'd abandoned their covers to strengthen Molembe's unit. The bouncers and band members brought their sophisticated weaponry with them. Saint-Denis and the Joyhouse Arkestra were ready to perform with nightscope and laser-locking Heckler & Koch MP-5 SDs.

Sharp and ready for battle hours ago, they were in danger of falling into that half-trance state that often came at the end of a long surveillance. Watching, waiting and staring so long that the stone walls seemed to move.

The fortress was in its third incarnation. When it was first built hundreds of years earlier, it had guarded Zandeville from the pirates and slavers plying the coast. Then it became a stronghold during the world wars, a place of refuge. In recent years, when Zandesi began to prosper and war seemed a distant concern, the ramshackle fortress was turned into a museum.

Across from the small parking lot and access road was a landscaped park. Garden hedges, bright flowers and gurgling fountains were spread among patches of palm trees, an idyllic symbol of Zandesi's prosperity. But now the idyll was inhabited by ZIS men with hellfire in their hands. Like serpents in the garden, Molembe thought.

The fortress was in its latest and probably last incarnation as a giant trap, a treasure house with counterfeit bullion.

"He won't come," Molembe stated, breaking the silence several minutes later as he stretched out his legs to ease his cramped muscles. "We haven't heard anything from the air base yet. Neither of the turncoat pilots have made a move. I think we guessed wrong."

"He'll come. He has no choice."

Molembe laughed. "There are several choices for Heinrich Fowler. Probably many we don't even know about it."

"Lots of choices," Bolan agreed. "But there's little chance he won't choose this one." He nodded toward the fortress. "He can run, he can surrender or he can try to make one last strike. He's still got his hard-core mercs with him, men who've fought alongside him for years. They're not the type to walk away. If Fowler does a fade, his rep fades with him. Believe me, they'll go for the gold."

Molembe nodded. He'd believed the same at one point in the evening. They'd baited the trap well.

But now he wasn't so sure. Now he could picture Fowler spiriting himself away, abandoning his men and settling for a hidden account somewhere. Men like Fowler prepared well for these things.

And so did Molembe.

He had the streets leading to the museum covered, and though the bay looked harmless with city lights painting their reflections on the water, ZIS cruisers were there as backup. The twin-hulled powerboats were manned by elite commandos, ready to hit the beach or troll for Fowler's mercs at sea.

Whichever way the German chose to come, they were ready.

"YOU CAN STOP right there," Captain Tsawa growled.

Both pilots turned. Suited up and ready for flight, they were only ten feet away from their Lynx chopper.

The younger pilot glanced longingly at the cockpit, as if he could teleport himself inside and escape. Then he looked back at the officer who'd leveled an automatic on him. "Julian," he whispered out of the side of his mouth, "what do we do?"

"We stop right there like the man says. What else can we do?"

His voice was resigned, as if he'd been expecting that sooner or later they'd be found out. But even as he spoke he turned slightly to his right, covering the slight motion of his hand dropping to his side arm.

Then he heard a click and looked up into the cold black eyes of a 12-gauge shotgun wielded by a tall ZIS man who stepped out from behind the chopper.

A second shotgunner appeared from the tail end of the chopper.

While the shock was still registering on the pilots, the cabin door slid open and a pair of uniformed officers jumped down to the tarmac, training their weapons on the pilots and disarming them.

"You boys are grounded," Captain Tsawa said as he approached Julian, keeping his automatic trained on him.

"What if we talk?" Julian asked.

Tsawa shrugged, his hard eyes boring into the pilot who'd tried to sell them out. "You can talk all you want, but there's damned little we don't already know about you and your movements, Julian. That's why you weren't allowed on the strike against Fowler's desert camp."

The pilot shook his head, trying to dispel the nightmare enfolding him.

"We've been watching you all along," Tsawa continued, "and we know where you were headed tonight."

The pilot laughed. "You a mind reader?"

"No," he said, "I'm a museum goer. Just like half of the ZIS. Tonight they're all waiting for the Fowler exhibition."

At the mention of the museum, Julian's heart sank. Then he looked dazed. No longer was he a pilot with information on Fowler to trade. Now he was just a traitor with little to offer. "How did you know?"

"Logic. Fowler had to have some reason to keep you alive for so long. Molembe figured it was so you could act as a taxi service when Fowler makes his final move. He loots the treasury, and you fly him out of the country. Then you all live happily ever after. That's the basic plan, isn't it?"

Julian nodded.

"Well, we're going to make some changes," Tsawa promised.

The copilot lost it then, talking wildly and asking for mercy, chanting a dozen excuses along with his promises to testify. He was looking for a way out of the trap that had been closing on them. "What can we do?"

Captain Tsawa smiled coldly. "There is one thing. In case Fowler contacts you for a security check, tell him all systems are go and you're on your way. But right now, take us through your flight plan for tonight. Every step of the way. Every contingency plan." He waved his automatic at the young pilot. "Any arguments?"

There were none.

A few minutes later Captain Tsawa radioed Martin Molembe. "The treasure hunt is on."

A CREAM-COLORED sports car drove along the road that followed the curves of the bay. About a quarter mile from the museum, it pulled off the road onto a wide stretch of soft shoulder, headlights spearing out toward the sea.

Then the lights flicked off.

Taken by itself, there was nothing remarkable about the incident. But then, separated by a few minutes, several other cars repeated the maneuver, slowly working their way down the stretch of road.

Fowler's men were arriving.

Backing up the seaside cars, a number of station wagons and vans began rolling down through the streets, heading toward the museum. Soon the convoy of killers was ready to strike.

Heinrich Fowler was in the lead van, chauffered by Gauclere.

The outside lights of the dockside museum had been shut off, and only a few windows gleamed brightly from the second floor. Three cars were in the parking lot, enough to make it look as if some guards and caretaker staff were on duty inside the museum.

Fowler looked over at Gauclere.

"Our last battle begins," he said. "Soon we'll be rich men again."

Gauclere nodded. He steadied his glasses and watched the front of the fortress. It was going to be a direct assault. Breach the walls, blow the vaults and make their getaway via chopper, which even now was heading their way. Gauclere had just received confirmation from the pilots.

"Let's hope we live to spend it," he grunted.

Fowler nodded. He stood, leaned over his seat and shouted into the back of the van. "Fire when ready."

The van doors slid open on both sides. Kneeling in position were two mercs with light antitank weapons on their shoulders. HEAT projectiles extended from the rear of the launch tubes. The LAW-80s were cocked and ready to fire.

The men fired their weapons in tandem. The bunker-busting rockets streaked through the air and thumped into the main entrance of the fortress. Wood, stone and iron shards flew into the air as the explosions shattered the night. Smoke clouds drifted out onto the fortress grounds.

Dark figures sprinted forward as the rest of Fowler's troops descended on the fortress. Firing on the run, they emptied full-auto bursts into the gaping opening and strafed the windows above.

The horde of gunners filtered throughout the building, some of them running up the stairs while other teams began a room-to-room seek-and-destroy on the ground floor. At the same time, a four-man demolition team of "bankers" hit the storage room that had been fortified and turned into a vault.

A shuddering roar swept throughout the fortress as C-4 plastique charges went off one after the other, unhinging the metal-reinforced doors of the vault and dropping them flat on the floor with a loud thud.

Then the bankers raced inside.

The heavy canvas that covered the stacks of bullion nearest the vault doors had been scorched and shredded by the blasts. And below the canvas, the counterfeit bullion was revealed. Streaks of gold paint had been burned off by the blast, revealing the iron beneath.

"It's fake," one of the men said. He stared at Fowler, who suddenly looked hypnotized.

The German turned away from the gold, slowly looking around him as if he could no longer recognize where he was. This was supposed to be his crowning moment, but he'd been duped, made to look a fool.

That point was struck home when Gauclere came running toward the vault. "There's no one here!" he shouted. "Not a single goddamn guard in the whole fucking place! A setup, dammit, it's a setup."

Molembe, Fowler thought. He'd been led here, and he'd blindly followed every step of the way.

"Come on!" Gauclere shouted, hammering Fowler on the shoulder, trying to drag him from the trance he'd fallen into. "Let's get the hell out of here before—"

Lightning bolts rocked the inside of the fortress. White searing blasts went nova, blinding and blasting the hardmen caught inside. Stun grenades and high-explosive rounds thumped through the breached entrance, through the smashed windows. Tear gas and acrid smoke turned the air into a choking cloud.

Fowler instinctively covered his eyes and staggered to one side of the room, waiting until the magnesium nova went away. Several seconds passed before he could see again.

THE ZIS COMMANDOS emerged from the trees and the gardens surrounding the front of the fortress. They came out firing, sending a fiery wall of machine-gun bursts and grenade blasts in front of them.

Grenade launchers kept up a steady barrage of stun and gas grenades. Molembe's blue berets opened up with Armsel Strikers, the automatic shotguns tearing into Fowler's lead van and punching jagged holes through the other cars in the mercenary convoy.

Bolan and Molembe spread out the line of commandos encircling the fortress, crouching and firing as they advanced.

Smoke, fire and screams poured out of every entrance. The entire fortress had become a booby trap.

FOWLER SHOUTED from the depths of his soul. It was a war cry that had had its birth generations ago and had echoed down through the ages. The Fowlers had been a proud family of warriors who'd cut their path across Europe and Africa, and wasn't supposed to end here in a godforsaken block house.

He clutched his Skorpion machine pistol.

The voice that had been shouting beside him suddenly became clear. It was Gauclere. He was jabbering about the chopper, telling him there was still a chance to escape if they could survive until the Lynx touched down.

"No chopper," Fowler said. "It won't be coming."

No transfer of gold had ever been made, he realized, even though his people had seen it made. Even Julian had witnessed the "transfer." "Even Julian," he murmured. The pilot had been deceived or captured, or he'd gone back over to the other side. It didn't matter. Even if Julian was still free, he wasn't the type of pilot to drop down in the middle of a free-fire zone.

The fortress shook on all sides as grenades and automatic fire thumped into it, reducing the walls and windows to rubble.

Fowler headed for the entrance to the fortress.

"Where are you going?" Gauclere shouted, tugging at his glasses as if they could help him see the

Heinrich Fowler he was accustomed to—Fowler the victor, not a Fowler in shock.

But Fowler was no longer listening.

He stepped out into the night. All around him he saw his men falling. Some of them dropped their weapons and put their hands over their heads.

A spiderweb of red lights darted through the night, coming from all sides. Laser sights, he realized. They'd prepared the ambush well.

He stood in front of the shattered entrance, his machine pistol hanging down at his side. Dark uniformed shapes bore down on him as a spot of laserlight knifed through the blackness. The red beam traveled up his chest, stopping at his breastbone.

"Drop your weapon!"

"Don't move!"

The shouts came from all around him, blending into one constant demand for his surrender.

Fowler looked down at the red dot, then shook his head and raised the machine pistol.

A half-dozen men opened fire before he could get off a shot. Fowler staggered back toward the fortress entrance, his arms thrown up over his head. Then he sagged to the ground, his dream of controlling Zandesi gone forever.

Gauclere dropped beside him, his glasses shattered and his skull shriven with bullets.

Bolan and Molembe lowered their weapons. All that remained now was the mop-up operation throughout the fortress grounds and a seaside villa north of Zandeville, where even now a fleet of ZIS cruisers was landing. In exchange for leniency, the turncoat pilots had revealed the location of Nashonge's comfortable prison.

Nashonge would stand trial or he'd die resisting capture. The choice was up to him.

Bolan felt a sense of satisfaction. Either way, Zandesi was free—the leadership of the Desert Knights had fallen.

This mission was over.

For the eternal soldier, Dan Samson, the battle has shifted to the Mexican-American war in Book 2 of the time-travel miniseries...

TIMERAIDER

John Barnes

Dan Samson, a hero for all time, is thrown back to the past to fight on the battlefields of history.

In Book 2: BATTLECRY, Dan Samson faces off against deadly enemies on both sides of the conflict—ready to forfeit his life to ensure the course of destiny.

Available in August at your favorite retail outlet.

Justice Marshall Cade and his partner, Janek, continue to bring home the law in Book 2 of the exciting new future-law-enforcement miniseries...

MIKE LINAKER

It takes a new breed of cop to deliver justice in tomorrow's America—a ravaged world gone mad.

In Book 2: HARDCASE, a series of seemingly random murders puts Cade and Janek on to a far-reaching conspiracy orchestrated by a ruthless money manipulator and military renegades with visions of taking over the U.S. government and military.

Available in September at your favorite retail outlet.

In the Deathlands, the only
thing that gets easier is dying.

JAMES AXLER

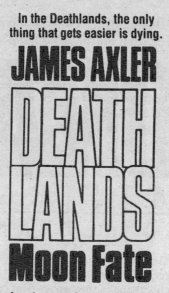

DEATH LANDS
Moon Fate

Out of the ruins of nuclear-torn America emerges a band of warrior-
survivalists, led by a one-eyed man called Ryan Cawdor. In their quest
to find a better life, they embark on a perilous odyssey across the ravaged wasteland known as Deathlands.

An ambush by a roving group of mutant Stickies puts Ryan in the clutches
of a tyrant who plans a human sacrifice as a symbol of his power. With
the rise of the new moon, Ryan Cawdor must meet his fate or chance
an escape through a deadly maze of uncharted canyons.

A twenty-first century commando meets his
match on a high-tech battlefield.

NOMAD
D E A T H   R A C E
D A V I D   A L E X A N D E R

He's called Nomad—a new breed of commando battling
the grim forces of techno-terrorism that threaten the
newfound peace of the twenty-first century.

In DEATH RACE, the second title in the NOMAD series,
the KGB is conspiring to bring America to her knees. A
supersoldier clone—Nomad's double—has been
programmed with a devastating termination directive.
Nomad becomes a hunted man in a cross-country death
race that leads to the prime target—the White House.